Matthew Delaney

nemesis

PRINTED AND BOUND IN THE UK.

PUBLISHED BY NEMESIS PUBLISHING LIMITED.

Cover art by Claire-Louise Clements

"Zeitgeist" Logo design by Matthew Delaney

ISBN: 978-1-909251-05-2

"Because it's never too late..."

ACKNOWLEDGEMENTS

With thanks to Mum, Claire, James P, James K, Michael, and Mick - whose continued support and encouragement made this work possible.

Also, additional special thanks goes to Claire for the fantastic artwork she provided for this project.

Chapter One

It all began on my 21st birthday. The one that never happened, at least not how it had *originally* happened, but anyway...

It had been a nice enough day, lacking in some respects but I was used to that by now. Sometimes life didn't always give us what we wanted and that's just the way it goes. Now before I continue, I feel I should explain how things were before all of this happened. It's important and sometimes even I forget.

The name's Luke. Luke Hudson. Compared to some I didn't have what you'd call a "normal" childhood but equally, compared to some others it wasn't as bad as it otherwise could have been. I'd been raised by my grandparents for as long as I could remember. Grandma Irene and Grandpa John. They were my Dad's parents and they were lovely.

Grandma Irene would always have her wispy white hair permed up and set and her eyes would always sparkle with life behind those thick rimmed glasses of hers. Above all else, Grandma Irene loved to paint – she did oil canvases mostly but her talent was undeniable and she was the type of person who could brighten the mood in a room just by walking into it – cheerfully singing songs from her youth. By comparison, Grandpa John was a bit more sedate – preferring to potter around in the garden when he wasn't indulging his love of military history by watching old movies or making scale models of tanks and battleships of varying sizes and descriptions. I was around the same height as him now, but I digress...they had raised me since I was three and had practically been the only family I had ever consciously known.

Things had happened when I was younger, when I had been *too* young to understand or remember and so the only family I had been left with were my grandparents. Well...and my Dad of course, but he was about as "part-time" as part-time Dads get. Dad, or James as he was otherwise known, had been detached for a long time – whatever had happened all those years ago had caused him to have a major breakdown that he'd never fully recovered from. I saw him every so often – usually when Grandma Irene or Grandpa John had forcibly reminded him that he was still a father and despite knowing that he wasn't well within himself I couldn't help but wish that he would make more of an effort. Whenever he had tried being a Dad he'd been pretty good at it but there was always an element to him, an unseen, unheard silent majority that closed him off from the rest of the world...and me, which ultimately led to him keeping his distance for prolonged amounts of time. I wanted to know him...to be close to him...I wanted him to be my Dad – the way it is for everyone else. But he just couldn't let anybody in, not even me.

Still, it could have been worse. At least I had a slim chance of getting to know Dad. I'd never known my Mum at all and I'd only ever seen her in a handful of old photographs. "Angie" they called her – that was her name. Although her name was literally the only detail either of my grandparents would ever choose to confess. It was like they couldn't bring themselves to talk about her. Sometimes Grandpa John would forget himself when I'd ask about her and start mumbling on incoherently – at which point Grandma Irene would look at him cautiously or cough insistently before adopting her stern tone of voice – *"Jonathan!"* she'd say, as if to warn him not to ramble on any further and he'd stop short of saying anything else.

It always puzzled me – *why* wouldn't they talk about her? *Why* wasn't I allowed to know more about my own Mum? It just seemed like another of those things in life I had no option but to get used to.

Anyway, that aside, everything started on that evening – the night of my 21st birthday, well...the *first* one...

Grandma Irene and Grandpa John had arranged a meal at 'The Red Pagoda' for my birthday which was well known as one of the finest and most expensive restaurants in town. The inside was an intricate and ornate collection of Chinese interior design and decorated lavishly in shades of red and gold. But despite being truly touched by the effort Grandma and Grandpa had gone to I couldn't help staring at the vacant seat at the four-person table and remember the missing guest. I didn't know what was worse – the fact that Dad hadn't shown up or the fact that I'd *known* he wouldn't. It was my 21st birthday and he was nowhere to be seen. Yet again he'd chosen to be absent from my life, leading me to wonder why.

Noticing my disappointment Grandma smiled sympathetically from across the table as she set her glasses back to the top of her nose.

"I'm sure he's got a good reason, darling." She soothed.

"...He bloody-well better have!" added Grandpa, huffing in frustration.

Getting a warning glance from Grandma for his undiplomatic candour, Grandpa retreated into sipping his glass of wine as the mood around the table steadily returned to normal.

"It's okay." I sighed.

It wasn't really but I didn't want to spoil the birthday meal that Grandma and Grandpa had gone to such effort to arrange. In many ways they felt like parents to me – more than my actual parents did anyway. Why was Dad so unable to be a proper Dad – like all my friend's Dads? For years I'd seen my friends all doing father-son things with their Dads and wished that I could have that kind of relationship with *my* Dad. It just wasn't fair.

The meal passed pleasantly after that – even without Dad showing up. Grandma and Grandpa recalled memories they had of me growing up in between reminding me how proud of me they were and it was good to see them smile. They had given up so much to raise me and I was eternally grateful to them – beyond grateful in fact – they were the only stable family I had ever known and I loved them immensely.

By far the biggest surprise was the cake – when the waitress placed it down on the table I stood in awe of the picture in front of me. It was a cake with a photo recreated on top – a photo I hadn't seen in a while – of me, Grandma and Grandpa in one of those studio-shot family photos and as I looked at it I felt divided. I treasured the memory that the photo invoked but at the same time I wished that it could have been Mum and Dad with me. And gazing at the dancing candle flames I briefly pondered all the birthdays that my parents had missed. A flame for each year and each year it hurt a little more.

"Go on Luke – make a wish, darling."

"Sure thing Grandma."

Deciding upon my wish I took a deep breath and blew each candle shy of its flame – with the wispy smoke lingering momentarily like an afterthought - carrying my silent request into the open air.

And then it happened.

Everything seemed to slow down to the extent where nearby conversations and movements blurred to a near-stop. I tried looking round in confusion, only to be rewarded with the sudden sensation of a lightning storm surging through my brain. It was like the onset of an extreme migraine. Suddenly my eyes retreated away from the growing intensity of nearby lights.

"Luke...Luke...are you okay, darling?" came Grandma's voice, though noticeably distorted as if delayed slightly out of time with my hearing it.

Dizzy. The feeling of movement despite my being still. Everything swirled and for the longest minute nothing seemed to make sense until the intense light flashed – leaving darkness in its all-consuming wake. And all at once I was no longer in the restaurant. In fact, I'm not quite sure *where* I was.

The first thing I remember after that is a pale light dancing radiantly through a small window as my eyes steadily opened and came into focus. I found myself laying on a sofa in what appeared to be a dimly-lit basement – served only by a single, dim light fitting that dangled from the ceiling a few feet away and got the impression that it was early evening although I'm not altogether sure *why* I felt that. Where was *this* place? Where were Grandma and Grandpa?

Sitting up I took note of my surroundings - finding (obviously) the old sofa that I was on, a large wooden cable reel that, now turned on its side, gave the impression of a makeshift coffee table, and a wooden staircase that swept around two walls on the far side of the room.

Suddenly the sound of footsteps from above caught me off-guard and I stood in anticipation of who was on the other end of the staircase. As the figure emerged ever steadily from the shadows beyond the light's embrace, I began to make out the figure coming down the stairs - a lady in her mid-thirties or so – with hair that reached the middle of her back. The closer the lady got the more she seemed to look like Grandma, only younger. But the similarities ended there as far as I could tell – this *wasn't* Grandma, so who on Earth was it?

"Glad you could join us sleepy head. For a moment there I thought you'd be out until nightfall. That must have been some headache." She smiled softly.

The headache. I remembered now. The restaurant – everything going...weird. But it was still all so hazy – like having woken up from a dream.

I touched my head instinctively where the pain had been most prominent. But it was gone. In fact, I didn't remember feeling it since I had opened my eyes a couple of minutes ago.

"What is this? Where am I?"

"Oh you poor dear, I know those headaches of yours can cause memory blanks. That must have been one hell of one if you don't remember where you are." She replied with genuine sympathy in her eyes, "You were helping your Uncle Henry clear out the basement when that headache of yours set-in. He was going to help you up to your room but you fell asleep on the sofa by the time he'd gone to get some tablets for you so we let you sleep it off."

It was a lot to take in and the harder I concentrated on what she had said the less seemed to make sense. Even though my mind felt as if it had just been on an extremely fast and nauseating rollercoaster, it still knew that something this lady was saying didn't seem right and yet her tone and body language had been consistently sincere. *She* believed what she was saying, so why didn't I?

"I...I don't have an Uncle Henry..." I replied eventually.

The lady looked shocked at first but soon cracked another smile and sighed gently with laughter under her breath.

"Don't be silly. Why, next you'll be telling me you don't know who *I* am either."

We studied each other's gaze carefully for a moment, in silent consideration as the next few seconds passed slowly by. I could tell from her, albeit sympathetic, expression that she seemed hurt at the thought of me not recognising her and what was even weirder was the twinge that shimmered throughout my chest at the sight of her looking upset, as if there was some kind of unspoken connection between us somehow. What was this? Who was she?

"Come on Luke, surely you remember me – Auntie Linda?"

A mere look in her eyes was enough to know that she'd be next to heartbroken if I said I honestly couldn't recognise her. But although not recognising her as an Aunt there *was* something inside of me – a small and unsubstantiated gut-instinct that believed she was who she claimed to be. It was the strangest case of heart clashing with head – each waging war upon the other in a furore of logic, memory and emotion.

"Of course I remember you."

I hated lying but I hated the thought of Linda being upset even more. What else could I have done?

Linda sighed with relief and put her arms around me lovingly which reinforced the feelings that she really *was* related to me – there was that family spark – that connection, despite me not knowing her. And in the fleeting seconds that she hugged me, the smell of her perfume conjured up sounds and images from deep inside my mind – showing them to me in an incoherent and distorted slide-show of vague, half-forgotten memories from early childhood. It was like a flashback only packed with all the power of a speeding freight train.

"You still feeling rough, sweetheart? Come on upstairs – I'll get you something to drink." Linda soothed.

There was something unmistakeably endearing about Linda, or "Auntie" Linda should I say, and the way in which she came across as so deeply caring. Ascending the sweeping staircase, we emerged in a modest yet homely kitchen and, true to her word, Linda made me a drink – which I sat and nursed at the small circular dining table as she pottered about preparing the evening meal.

It was all so strange like a dream only more coherent. The drinking glass in front of me on the table was cold to the touch just as it should be; the table felt just as solid as it should have done and the textured smells escaping from the oven evoked the same sensation of appetite and anticipation as they would have anywhere else. Where was this place? Where had I woken up? Where were Grandma and Grandpa?

Getting up, I wandered into the hallway – observing the photos hanging on the wall: Linda with a man and a boy who I guessed had to be "Uncle" Henry and their son – whom Auntie Linda had referred to as Josh when she had been making me a drink; Grandma and Grandpa looking noticeably younger – posing in front of the Golden Gate Bridge in San Francisco;

and...a younger version of Dad sitting next to a younger Linda each grinning widely while on a train. The more I looked, the more that younger version of Dad reminded me of the reflection I was always greeted by in the mirror and if I'm honest, part of me hated myself for acknowledging the similarity. There was something undeniably melancholy about looking like a relative you barely knew – like you were some forgotten echo that looked the part but always appeared immeasurable when compared to the real McCoy. Grandma in particular was forever telling me how much I resembled my Dad when he had been my age. I guess she was trying to help make me feel closer to him but all it really did was irritate me – after all, why would I want to be like him – always so detached, bitter and insular? He always seemed to shut me out – so why would I ever want to become that?

All this thinking about Dad and my feelings on our less than perfect relationship led me to look for a distraction – preferably of the alcoholic variety and, peering into the living room I found a small and tremendously dated bar in one corner of the room. Needless to say I acquainted myself with it immediately and rummaged through the modest collection of bottles stashed snugly on one of the shelves – eventually settling for a generous tumbler of whiskey on the rocks. I looked around the reasonably cosy living room in greater detail as my lips kissed the smooth glass and welcomed the whiskey to the party until, that was, a voice exploded from the doorway.

"What the hell do you think you're doing?!"

I turned round, shocked, as the imposing figure of "Uncle" Henry loomed a few feet away – apparently ready to charge across the room at me at a moment's notice. His expression was a far cry from the smile he'd worn in the family portrait and it was clear that I wasn't going to enjoy the rest of my drink in peace.

As it turned out, Uncle Henry was taller than I had anticipated – mid thirties with oval-rimmed glasses and a stubbly brown beard that sat comfortably beneath his surprisingly plentiful head of hair. His voice carried a natural and definitive air of authority and, I thought, was commanding enough to make trees stop swaying in the breeze. Henry's stance made it clear that he meant business and that to most people, myself included, he would be formidable opposition if challenged.

"I'm having a drink." I answered candidly; unaware as to why Henry had such a problem with me drinking.

"Yes I can see that." He replied before raising his voice and shouting into the hallway, "LINDA!"

I didn't understand what the problem was – perhaps this guy was just overly protective of his drinks cabinet or something. Either way, I was slowly learning to expect 'weird' as the norm round here – wherever the hell 'here' actually was.

As we stood in silence awaiting the imminent arrival of Auntie Linda, I dared to tempt another sip of whiskey between my lips which, apart from being personally satisfying, served only to infuriate Uncle Henry further who promptly intensified his glare and motioned for me to put the tumbler down on the side. Needless to say I continued to cradle the tumbler in one hand as we waited.

True enough, Auntie Linda emerged in the doorway mere seconds later looking bewildered at Henry's impromptu and unflattering summons.

"Henry...what is it? What's all the commotion?"

"That!" Henry exclaimed while pointing dramatically towards me and the offending glassware.

Linda looked stunned but nowhere near as close to going into orbit as Henry. She stepped towards me – wearing a warm and disarming smile that you couldn't help but feel entranced by. Linda lifted the tumbler from my hand and, to my surprise; I didn't offer any resistance though I didn't know why. Once she'd placed the tumbler down Linda put a loving arm around me and laughed under her breath.

"Oh Luke, you know that's off limits. That's only for the grownups."

By this point I was hopelessly confused. It was like I had woken up in a different world where my name was the only certainty amidst the surreal environment I'd found myself immersed in. Either that or I was being seriously set up for a TV show. Needless to say I was praying for the latter because the thought that this was *really* happening was just too strange.

"...'grownups'? What do you mean? I'm 21. How much more grown-up am I supposed to get?!"

In the instant I had finished that sentence I knew that this was no joke – they weren't toying with me and it was clear from their bemused expressions that I might have well answered them in a foreign language for all the good my statement seemed to carry with them. What was going on?

"21?! Whatever gave you that idea darling?" Linda smiled softly.

"Well twenty-years plus a birthday cake *kinda'* gave it away." I answered glibly.

"Oh Luke, that must have been some bump to the head. You're only fifteen sweetheart."

"And in this house fifteen year olds do *not* get to sample alcohol." added Henry.

Now it was my turn to gaze unconvincingly at them. What they were saying was ludicrous. I *was* 21. I had been with Grandma and Grandpa in the restaurant celebrating. I had blown out the candles and then everything after that was a blur until I woke up here in this place.

Stunned by how serious their claims were expressed I glanced curiously into the small mirror hanging on the wall – desperate for it to give *my* claim some tangible validity. To prove that I was 21 and not 15 as they were suggesting. It just wasn't possible. But then my reflection gazed back at me – a slightly younger face than the one I remembered seeing when I'd been getting ready for the restaurant. That face – it *was* me but me at fifteen. I lightly probed my face with my fingers as I continued studying the impossible reflection in the mirror, unsure of what to think or feel. What was happening?

Now it was official – this simply could *not* get any weirder. It just wasn't possible. It felt like I'd dropped into *'The Twilight Zone'* as it was.

"Alright," I laughed, though unsure why I found any of this amusing at all, "So if I'm fifteen then what year is it?"

"Well...1990 of course, what year did you think it was?" answered Linda.

I stood corrected. This wasn't weird - *this* was off the chart.

Chapter Two

I spent the rest of that evening trying to make sense of all this and spent the entire *night* trying to convince myself that this was all some crazy, lucid dream. But by the time morning rolled around and shone through the curtains I still found myself in the same place. *This* place. *This* 1990.

It was just too much to believe – I had barely been a year old in 1990 so why was I now here and fifteen years old? It felt like I had been robbed of a birthday and dropped into some surreal alternate reality. It was a strange place - and it didn't look to be getting any less strange anytime soon.

"Rise and shine sleepy head." boomed a motherly yet overly-enthusiastic voice, waking me with a start as daylight flooded mercilessly into the room.

Reacting to the sudden shattered serenity I leapt upwards into a seated position – only to be momentarily dazzled by the intense change in light and scrambled for cover – retreating back under the duvet. Having regrouped, I eventually poked my head out from the cosy hiding place to see "Auntie" Linda looking back at me with a smile that could light up half the national grid.

"Woah...what the hell?! What are you doing? It's only..." I paused for a second as I winced at the digital alarm clock on the bedside table and waited for the green digits to come into focus, "...7am?! You're expecting me to get up at 7am?! We've gotta talk!"

I couldn't believe it. My head was telling me this wasn't happening – that I was still asleep – having passed out in the restaurant – but my eyes kept on reminding me that, for now at least, I was anchored here – in 1990, with family I never knew I had. This was all so weird and it was hard to acclimatise – every time I came close to being at peace with this place, something else revealed itself to me and threw everything back into a state of flux.

"Well, there'll be plenty of time to talk over breakfast. Now hurry up and get ready – there's some toiletries for you in the bathroom and your uniforms in the wardrobe."

"Uniform?! What do I need a uniform for?"

"For school of course, now come on – chop, chop." Linda offered cheerfully before leaving the room and closing the door behind her.

In the wake of her leaving the room my eyes froze open in sheer disbelief. As I got up and walked across to the wardrobe I prayed that I had misheard her or that she had been joking. But as I opened out the double doors to the wooden wardrobe it was plain to see that she had been completely serious as there, hanging in front of me, was the neatly ironed school uniform – black trousers and blazer, the latter of which was proudly emblazoned with the school's purple-clad emblem; a white shirt; grey socks; and a purple and black diagonally-striped tie. I stared at it – hoping it would go away – hoping that I'd wake up back in the restaurant with Grandma and Grandpa around me but no such event came. None of this made sense but, again, I felt no choice but to (begrudgingly) play along until some answers came my way which, judging by recent events could be some considerable time.

There was so much I wanted to say. Profanity mostly. But instead, having summoned some semblance of resolve, I sighed and got dressed as Linda had asked.

School had been "difficult" for me to say the least – the first time round that is, not *this* weirdness. Growing up without Dad (for the most part) and Mum (at all) had been really tough although I'd never usually allow myself to admit it. Grandma and Grandpa had always done their best but the absence of my parents had always gotten to me – like a poison that grows stronger over time. They say that absence makes the heart grow fonder but in this instance it was more a case of absence makes the heart grow colder. School had been an ongoing battle of endurance – teased for the most part for allegedly being 'unwanted' as well as being ridiculed for preferring to work hard instead of goofing around had left me hardened and slightly bitter...okay, fine – **very** bitter but it all served to make me more self-sufficient and independent – after all, why rely on others when all they do is let you down?

As I gazed at the now fully clothed reflection in front of me I flashed back to some of the more memorable clashes I had had with authority back at school, as I did up my tie. They had branded me disruptive because I had refused point-blank to be a willing victim of the crap I'd been continually dealt and in return I had branded *them* incompetent and impotent at allowing the problem to exist in the first place, not to mention letting it carry on for as long as it did. Needless to say that there was no great love lost on either side and that school – especially high school – had largely been a source of conflict as much as education.

By the time I went downstairs for breakfast everyone else had finished. In fact Uncle Henry had even left for work – leaving Auntie Linda lovingly embracing a steaming cup of what smelt like coffee and Josh playing a handheld games console.

"Good morning Luke. Aww – don't you look smart." She remarked affectionately.

"Trust me – there are *no* words to describe this scene." I answered, flatly.

While pouring out a bowlful of cereal I took notice of how real everything felt and appeared. If this was a dream then it was the most lucid and realistic one I ever remember having. But for all my secret yearning of waking back up in 2010, my gut instinct was telling me that this was for real – no dream could ever be this coherent – it just wasn't possible, there was too much detail, too much stark realism. Trust me, if I had a dog I'd be telling it that we were about as far from Kansas as any cartographer could ever imagine.

Despite my obvious objections to what was happening, Auntie Linda remained her warm, cheerful, motherly self as she took her place at the table whilst lovingly taking stray sips from her coffee cup.

"You'll feel better once you settle in, dear. The first few days are always the hardest." She soothed over a reassuring smile.

For a moment I pondered the ambiguity of what she had said – was she talking about school or this place? The thought of Linda *knowing* where I'd come from flashed across my mind. Did she know? Or was I making connections that weren't valid? I couldn't tell and so, undecided on which way to take what she had said, I merely smiled weakly in response as I poured the milk over the cornflakes.

As I ate breakfast at the table, surrounded by family I didn't know I had until yesterday, I tried observing as much as I could about this place. If was going to be here for some time, and I got the feeling I was, then I knew I needed to be clued-up on where (not to mention *when*) I was. While Linda drank her coffee in near-silence and I ate my cornflakes, the only sound to grace the room was the musical chirping coming from Josh's handheld games console.

"Josh, how many times have I told you that that thing doesn't belong at this table?" Linda exclaimed authoritatively, having grown noticeably irritated by the constant chirping.

"But..."

"No 'buts' mister."

And with that Linda gently lifted the console out of Josh's hands, turned it off and placed it on the counter behind her. It was only then, as it was in transit, that I got a clear view of it and recognised it from my (actual) youth.

"Hey, is that a Gameboy? An *original* Gameboy? Man, I haven't seen one of those in years." I mused, vaguely remembering the one I'd got for my sixth birthday.

Josh's face suddenly crinkled up in confusion as he turned to me, gazing at me as if I had said something outrageous.

"Years?! I got that for Christmas. And what d'ya mean 'original'?"

"Well...they came out in what? '89?" I retorted in-between spoonfuls of cereal.

"Yeah – which would make it 1990 *now*. Geez – how hard did you hit your head?!"

No sooner had Josh finished, I instantly felt baffled. It had been such an obvious faux-pas but if there had been any part of me that had forgotten that this was allegedly 1990 then it had just been forcibly reminded. And despite having heard it so many times it still seemed impossible to get my head around. You don't just black-out in one year and wake up twenty years earlier, although clearly I *had*. All that remained now was to work out why. After all, the whole notion of me being a twenty-one year old teenager in a time when (in reality) I had only just been approaching my first birthday was enough to perplex even the most vivid of imaginations. It was beyond belief and yet here I was and I suppose it was just something I'd have to get to grips with if there was to be any chance of finding out just what on Earth was going on and, more importantly, how to get home.

Josh and I left for school soon after that – with Josh leading the way through the vaguely familiar streets and having to (begrudgingly) keep stopping when I did to observe certain sights. So much was different in *this* version of the town compared to the one I was used to – housing developments that hadn't been built yet; independent shops that still stood where chain stores were destined to take their place and models of cars that I hadn't seen in such abundance in a long time. It was like a living, breathing time capsule and, despite my reservations about being here, was quite spectacular.

"Would you hurry up?! You're acting like you haven't seen any of this before."

"I haven't. Not like *this* anyway." I replied absently, much to Josh's confusion.

It was quite honestly the weirdest thing I could ever recall. In many ways I suppose it was like (literally) walking through a living photo-album – seeing a world in the flesh that up until now had been confined to a handful of photos and my grandparents' vague recollections of how things had been around the time I was born.

After turning a corner next to a petrol station Josh waved to a girl waiting beside a wall a hundred yards or so away.

"Ok," he said quietly, "there's Charlotte. Don't say anything weird, alright?"

"What – like Martians are coming to invade the Earth? Or that the world *is* flat after all?" I teased.

Josh scowled briefly – looking momentarily like a B-movie villain as he affirmed the seriousness of what he had said. Holding my hands up in a 'surrender' gesture, I acknowledged that I'd go along with what he'd said although to be fair, Josh's B-movie villain stare had been quite funny and I had been tempted to drag it out a bit longer.

It was as Josh and Charlotte were greeting each other that I noticed my cousin seemed extremely caught-up about how to act around Charlotte, leading me to wonder whether Josh felt something deeper for her. In fact I quickly became convinced that Josh had a thing for Charlotte and that, without her giving too much away, Charlotte felt something similar for him.

"Who's this, Josh?" she asked softly.

"Charlotte this is Luke, my cousin. He's staying with us for a while."

Despite knowing that she hadn't expected to see me, there was still something odd about the way Charlotte looked at me as she absorbed what Josh had told her. Don't get me wrong, she wasn't being rude and she held a pleasant expression on her face the entire time but there was something in her gaze that just seemed to notice I was out of place – like I didn't belong. It was weird and hard to explain but...I dunno – it just seemed odd.

"Hey Luke." Charlotte smiled thinly, with a twinkle in her eye.

"Hi."

Charlotte was just shorter than Josh and had frizzy, fluffy golden brown hair arranged very stylishly with the aid of a butterfly clip. Her eyes and smile were enough to make anyone feel at ease and it was clear that she cared a lot for Josh. It was also easy to tell why Josh liked her so much – after all, she was obviously a relaxed, caring person and Josh seemed like a good judge of character so who was I to argue?

We carried on walking towards the school after that – with Josh and Charlotte blissfully chatting away among themselves while I trailed silently alongside deep in thought. I thought about Grandma and Grandpa – where were they? Were they alright? No doubt they'd be worried about me. For as long as I could remember they had been the only two people that had never let me down. I wished that there was some way I could tell them I was alright even if I was stuck in 1990. For all of my faults and scrapes I'd got into over the years they had always been there for me and they had never stopped loving me. They were the only stable family I knew, especially with Dad doing a disappearing act every chance he got.

"So Luke," Charlotte asked suddenly, catching me off-guard, "Where are you from?"

I stumbled for words to answer her with as she brushed a rogue strand of frizzy brown hair back behind her left ear. I suppose I could have lied and made something up on the spot but somehow I couldn't bring myself to lie to Charlotte. It was the strangest thing – I just simply could not lie to her. Confused at how best to answer without sounding crazy or sending Josh into orbit by being "weird", I tried giving a truthful answer that wouldn't sound out of place.

"I...grew up in Lavender Hill." I answered honestly.

"Oh – nice. I hear some of those places have their own bus stops to get from one end of the driveway to the other."

Laughing, I pictured at once the houses that Charlotte was referring to – the large Victorian houses that adorned a lot of the well-kept streets in that area. Grandma and Grandpa's house was more modest than those ones but despite not being a suburban mansion it was home, *my* home, and I missed it. But more than that, I missed Grandma and Grandpa. I hoped they were alright.

"Well, we don't have our own bus stop but we *do* have a cat called Elvis."

Charlotte laughed, "*Elvis*, huh? Cool."

The arrival at the school was like walking back into a bad dream – I'd spent so long fighting all manner of classroom tyrants and self-styled playground dictators that my view of school had become rather jaded. For me it wasn't so much a place of learning but a moral battlefield – fighting to the last inch for what I believed in amidst a micro-world that didn't care. Uniformed conformity was demanded and I hated it. It failed to account for the individual – failed to nurture the talent of the individual – preferring instead to deliver a 'one-size fits all' education. And if, for whatever reason, you didn't happen to fit that one-size then you had two choices – fight or be forgotten.

From where the three of us stood just outside the main gate it was clear to see what was unfolding throughout the exterior of the school – groups of teenagers running about, some playing ballgames; other smaller cliques gathering for some clandestine gossip catch-up session; and the teenage playground dictators who much like lions in a pride were strikingly asserting their dominance over the more introverted of those assembled.

"Right where we left it." Josh laughed lightly, obviously having become accustomed to the scene in front of us.

"I think I'm in Hell." I remarked, seemingly frozen to the spot in mild despair.

With that, Charlotte put one arm around my shoulders and gently tugged me off my static standpoint.

"Come on, it's not *that* bad." She said.

Something in Charlotte's friendly manner convinced me to cross the threshold of the school gate with her and Josh. It felt so alien walking back into high school again – especially as a student. The bell for morning registration rang soon after we arrived – calling to those here assembled much like a church bell summons a congregation – and so the teenage horde began filtering their way through doors to different buildings throughout the site. Auntie Linda had told me that I was in Josh's form just before we'd left the house earlier so I stuck close to him – having to push through moving walls of people at some points just to keep up with him until eventually we arrived at the form room door. From the look of the inside it looked like a geography classroom – with colourful maps and landscape cross-sections proudly adorning the walls.

"Come on, she'll throw a fit if we're late."

I paused, still uneasy with having to go along with all of this. It was all so strange – so far removed from comprehension that I honestly didn't know what to do. But I knew that I had to keep up the pretence in this world – this place if I was to stand any chance of seeing Grandma and Grandpa again – not to mention 2010 and so, boosting my waning morale with a deep breath, I decided to just go with the flow – for now at least, and walked into the classroom alongside Josh. After all, what's the worst that could happen?

* * *

"Get out! Get out of my classroom at once!"

Incredible – it was only 10am on my first day here and already I was in trouble for yet again locking horns with authority. I'd made it to second period without something happening which was definitely a personal best. Now, don't get me wrong – in no way am I what they'd call "anti-authority" or anything like that. After all, authority did have its place and its uses but in my opinion there was a major difference between authority *having* its place and authority *knowing* its place. From how I'd learnt to see things, authority was impotent without respect and respect was earned – never demanded. With the exception of my grandparents, all my life I'd been confronted by representations of authority that demanded things of me without first having earned my respect – always demanding that I conform to an ideal even if it trampled upon how I felt. Where was the respect in that? Needless to say that *this* encounter measured up perfectly with my less-than flattering opinion of such stringent and cavalier authority. I guess the blackboard dictator wanted me to stand outside the classroom and think about how sorry I was but screw that – why should I care what someone who doesn't even know me thinks? As it turned out, I only managed to take my little protest a few feet down the corridor before a voice boomed after me – echoing off the otherwise silent walls.

"Hudson – where on Earth do you think you're going?! Come back here at once."

Part of me wanted to keep on walking – just keep on putting one foot in front of the other until this oppression was far behind me but there was that defiant streak in me that craved for a settled score – refusing to leave things as they were and so I turned to confront the red-faced teacher.

He was taller than he'd seemed in the classroom – but only a little. Middle-aged, it was easy to see from the determination in his eyes and the receding hairline that he was an evidently battle-scarred veteran of these corridors – the type of teacher that looks as if they've been at a school since time began. The presence of his bushy black moustache twitching in anticipation made the showdown seem like some budget western – with each of us trading loaded looks at the other.

"First of all, 'Hudson' is my surname and it is generally considered rude to address someone as such without the prefix of 'mister'. And second, in answer to your question, I'm going anywhere as long as it's away from you."

At this stage, having said my peace, I was prepared to leave it at that and so turned to walk away again until a firm hand grabbed my arm tightly – stopping me from going any further. Apparently the moustache-wearing blackboard dictator wasn't quite finished with me, and I braced myself for the inevitable counter-strike.

"I don't know where you've come from or who you think you are but at this school students listen to teachers." He hissed.

"Oh I'm listening, 'sir', I just don't like what you're saying." I answered, scowling in response.

"Is that right? Why don't you repeat that to the headteacher?"

It was a classic trick, some might even say textbook — to threaten someone with the unquantifiable wrath of higher authority and I suppose those not hardened to this type of power-play would, at this stage, back down and offer their unconditional surrender. But I had a different approach — in these types of situations I tended to side with the argument that I was already in trouble — so why not continue to fight on until the odds or opposition demanded otherwise? In my opinion, it was better to fight and go down fighting than to surrender at the first hurdle and never fight at all. Life was all about survival and survival was nothing without the determination to overcome that which stands in your way.

"Well that sure as hell beats standing here making polite conversation with you. Lead on." I retorted definitely, motioning for him to lead the way.

True to his word, the blackboard dictator (real name Mr Carson, by the way) marched me straight to the headteacher's office and dramatically recounted our exchange with all of the emphasis and flare of a stage-school pro to an extent where even I thought he should be nominated for some manner of award. When he was finished he left me to the mercy of the headteacher — Mrs Burridge, after having been personally assured by her that she would deal with the situation. Carson offered me a disapproving parting glance before finally leaving the room and then there were two.

"Take a seat Luke." she said softly.

I didn't know how to interpret Mrs Burridge at this point but nevertheless chose to comply until reason persuaded me otherwise. Was she genuinely being courteous or was this one of those 'false sense of security' things? Either way I played along and waited for Burridge to show her hand.

She looked close to retirement – with her white hair arranged in a very commanding bun that sat atop her head. Mrs Burridge considered the world through half-moon glasses which, when not in use, rested comfortably on the end of a chain that she wore around her neck. And for a fleeting moment I could have sworn I noticed a hearing-aid behind her right ear as she tilted her head slightly while reaching into one of her desk drawers for something before returning her attention to the matter at hand.

"Well, as first days go you haven't exactly got off to a perfect start. Why do you think that is?" she asked calmly while taking her glasses off and holding them by one end.

"I don't know...I don't know *why* I'm here. What am I supposed to *do*? Who am I supposed to *be*? I just want to go home."

Mrs Burridge considered me carefully as if examining a part of me beneath what the rest of the world saw – a part that went deeper than skin. She momentarily flicked through a few pages of a file, presumably mine, that rested on her desk before raising her head to address me again.

"Yes, I see from your records that you're staying with your Aunt and Uncle at the moment. All this change must be hard for you." Burridge offered compassionately.

Was this a trick? *Was* she trying to find some clandestine way to reach the 'me' that lived beneath the surface of all this murky rage and angst? But for all of my cautionary thoughts, I couldn't help but be calmed by the courteous and respectful manner in which she spoke to me.

Sighing, half in humour, I pondered the stark accuracy of Mrs Burridge's last statement without her having known the true depth of my situation.

"It must be hard for you being away from your parents like this." She continued.

"Not really – I've never really had parents to miss, or to miss me."

"Everyone has parents, Luke."

"Yeah but most people have parents who want them. All I've got is a Mum that disappeared off the face of the Earth and a Dad that rarely takes the time to acknowledge I even exist." I recounted frankly.

I'd never really said that out loud before or been that brutally frank. Sure, I'd thought it a million times over but up till now it had never been able to escape the confines of my thoughts. It brought a tear to one eye and hurt to confess the depth of my detached relationship with my parents to the open world. I guess everyone needs to feel close to the people that made them – that gave birth to them and raised them but it was different in my case, as much as I wished otherwise. Things had happened that prevented me having that relationship that most people take for granted and that was a bitter pill to keep on swallowing.

Mrs Burridge and I spoke for some time after all and to my surprise she earned my respect pretty quickly. She asked me (quite nicely I might add) to give myself a fair chance to settle in – both at school and at home...well, Linda's house.

We talked about my hardened view on authority and, again to my surprise, Mrs Burridge seemed to genuinely empathise with a lot of the stuff I'd been through – at least the stuff I could tell her without her thinking I had lost my mind anyway. And after all that, she offered me a choice...

"Now then, about earlier. I *could* give you a detention *or* you could apologise to Mr Carson – it's up to you. Which would you prefer?"

From her tone it was clear that there was no element of sarcasm or menace to her words – her statement hadn't been rhetorical. She was being sincere and I appreciated being spoken to like I mattered – like somebody cared.

"I'll apologise. He's only doing his job, right?"

Mrs Burridge looked over at me and nodded approvingly – like we had reached a point where we were on the same wave length. With that said I was then told I was free to go (to whatever lesson I'd been timetabled to go to that is).

"Oh, and Luke," she said as I neared the door, "Are you related to a *James* Hudson at all?"

I stopped and turned back to face her whilst considering my reply. In an instant the mention of Dad brought my real life flooding back to the fore-front.

"Sort of." I replied awkwardly.

"I thought so. You're just like he was at that age. It must be in the blood."

In truth I didn't know what I should or even *could* say in response and so replied only with a silent smile. I wanted to be close to him but at the same time I hardly knew him. To me, James Hudson was an enigma – one which I felt I could easily spend a lifetime trying to solve and it was difficult whenever people compared us because as much as I felt some connection to him, I was scared of *becoming* like he was – scared of becoming alone.

Thankfully after that the rest of the day passed by without incident and without inadvertently upsetting any more of the faculty. It was strange being back in a school environment again – that regime, that structure, those endless lessons you don't feel you'll ever need to use 'in the real world'. And although I had to sit through one of the most painful maths lessons I've ever endured as well as a design and technology lesson with a teacher that looked and spoke with all the enthusiasm of a mad scientist, it was balanced by having geography and art which I'd always had a keen interest in and which had never failed to be a breath of fresh air, providing some measure of respite from the furore of the rest of academia.

Josh was already in the form room when I arrived for afternoon registration and he immediately began quizzing me about the earlier incident with Carson which by now had become amusingly exaggerated by the student rumour-mill.

"So I heard you gave Carson a run for his money." He said, eagerly waiting for more information.

I laughed – amused by how exaggerated something small could become in a matter of hours.

"We disagreed on a couple of things and I lost my temper – it's nothing to be proud of."

It was acclaim of the worst kind – that incident with Mr Carson had been born from a moment of anger – a moment I regretted having and yet it had been interpreted by others as representative of who I was and I hated that. That wasn't me – I wasn't some angry young hell-raiser. I got annoyed at things and was, on occasions, perhaps too vocal on certain matters for my own good but I wasn't the person people kept seeing me as. I wasn't guided by anger but rather overwhelmed by it on occasion. I wasn't proud of that fact but it was true. Anger was a part of who I'd become but it wasn't all I was or even all I could be. It just seemed infuriatingly shallow that people only recognised something that was skin-deep.

"That's not how I heard it."

"Well...you heard it wrong, okay. Can we drop this now please?" I replied, trying to curtail my frustration at being misunderstood.

"Sure." Josh answered, taken aback by my reaction.

When the bell chimed we left the block our form room was in having merged involuntarily with the teenage stampede trying to escape the confines of the building and it was only as we emerged in the open that I saw Mr Carson on duty as the stampede thinned out after leaving the captivity of the corridor. He was on duty overseeing the home-time rush and I knew that now was the opportune time to deliver on my promise to Mrs Burridge and so swallowing my pride I prepared to make good on my word.

"Wait for me at the gate, okay?" I said, turning to Josh.

"Why?"

"Cos' there's something I've gotta do first."

Josh looked round and spotted Mr Carson before cracking a wry smile, "Oh I see – round two is it?!"

I rolled my eyes before forcibly, yet playfully, guiding him in the direction of the gate, "Just be a good boy and wait at the gate. Go on – shoo!"

Bemused, Josh walked off towards the main gate as I cautiously stepped towards Mr Carson, unsure of how I'd be received.

"Excuse me...Mr Carson. Can I have a word with you please?" I asked humbly.

Carson looked suspicious at first - with his bushy moustache twitching with uncertainty his stance softened slightly.

"Sure."

"About earlier...I was angry about some stuff I've got going on and I guess I took what you said the wrong way. I guess what I'm trying to say is that...I'm sorry we got off to a bad start."

"We all have bad days, son, its how we learn from them that matters because *that* kind of education can't be taught."

"Well, thanks for hearing me out."

"No problem. Now go home Mr Hudson – I have a pint of bitter and barstool with my name on it waiting for me. The quicker you kids leave the quicker I can be reunited with 'em."

*   *   *

After that the next few hours seemed blissfully sedate – like having swallowed my pride and apologising to Mr Carson had somehow brought me more in tune with this place – it was the strangest thing but this place was becoming less and less alien – in a spooky sort of way it was beginning to feel almost like home.

Back at Auntie Linda's house, the late afternoon seamlessly melted into early evening and Linda was soon announcing that dinner was ready – pre-empting the gathering around the kitchen table minus Uncle Henry who was apparently working late. As we communed together we each shared aspects of our day as Auntie Linda led the light-hearted conversation. Even now I could see parallels between Linda and Grandma Irene who always did something similar. It was the subtle art of keeping a family connected with one-another – that each member contributed to making a whole and was thoroughly enrapturing as the genuine warmth surrounded you and warmed even the coldest extremes of a person.

I was mortified when Josh mentioned my run-in with Mr Carson and added his characteristic flare to the re-telling and expected to have to defend myself against a torrent of judgement but instead Linda calmly asked me for my less dramatised account of what had happened and lightened sympathetically when she learned that I'd voluntarily apologised.

"Well done Luke. That took character. I'm proud of you." she'd said whilst twisting her fork around another clump of spaghetti bolognaise.

The doorbell chimed barely a few minutes after we'd finished eating. Auntie Linda was mid-way through carrying some of the used crockery carefully to the sink while Josh had once again become immersed in the handheld video game he was currently battling through and as such remained oblivious to the outside world.

"I'll get it." I offered cheerfully.

"Thank you Luke." Linda called back as she began running the tap for the washing up.

Apart from the whole being stuck in 1990 thing, things seemed to be going quite well despite my growing yearning to see Grandma and Grandpa again. Ever since I'd first woken up in the basement I had hoped, if-not prayed, that the reason I was here would make itself apparent. But perhaps I should have learnt to have been more careful what I wished for as, opening the front door, I was confronted with a sight I never previously thought I'd see.

"Who is it Luke?"

"It's...*them*." I answered quietly – more to myself than anyone else.

As Auntie Linda made her way to the front door – with tea towel firmly in hand I stood frozen in disbelief as I continued to gaze at the scene directly in front of me. There, standing in the doorway, was Dad - looking noticeably younger and carrying a baby carrier in one hand whilst standing next to a slim young woman who up until now I had only known as Angie...

June 1996 (Aged 7)

I guess I must have only been about seven when it happened. I'd woken up late one evening and started heading downstairs where either Grandma or Grandpa would make me a warm milky drink and tell me stories until I fell asleep again. But this time was different. I'd only descended about four or five steps when the sound of raised voices glued me to the spot. It wasn't the TV – the voices were too clear and familiar for that. They sounded like they were coming from the kitchen and if the tone was anything to go by – it was serious. I remember clinging to the soft blue elephant teddy that I took everywhere when I was younger – holding it tight and rubbing my eyes with my other hand just to prove to myself that I wasn't dreaming; that this was actually happening.

With the kitchen door only slightly ajar I had to remain super quiet in order to make out the conversation...

"You can't be serious! I don't think you've thought this through." announced Grandma.

She sounded serious – one of her "telling off" tones – one without a single trace of humour to be found. Next to speak was Grandpa and it didn't sound like he was in a joking mood either.

"You've got responsibilities here son. You can't just walk away."

"I'll send money."

"James it's not about the money and you know it. Your son needs you. You can't just up and leave. He'll be heartbroken. He barely sees enough of you as it is." Grandma shot back.

"Exactly. It'll be better for him if I go now. I can't do it. I want to but I just can't. I can't face him knowing that she..."

Dad's words had become slightly broken – as if he was fighting back tears or a lump in his throat just to utter them aloud. I didn't understand what was going on or why. Why was Dad so upset and why did he want to go away?

"She was six years ago, son. You've got to pull yourself together and get on with your life; for Luke's sake as much as yours."

"But every time I look at him I see her. It's just too much. I can't stand seeing the disappointment in his eyes but I can't get close to him without thinking of Angie. It tears me apart. I thought...that things were going to be different and then..."

"Look, James, Luke is as much your son as he is Angie's; and you have a responsibility – even more so in Angie's absence."

The argument continued to rage on as I kept hearing Dad reiterate how much he wanted to leave; with each word cutting right through me – ripping shards of my childhood innocence with the strength of his conviction. He wanted to move away for good. Forever. It hurt more than any pain I felt before or since and at that moment I didn't know whether to cry or scream.

The kitchen door opened – sending a thin strip of light pouring down the length of the hallway.

"I knew you wouldn't understand." said Dad as his silhouette broke the perfect shape of the light.

He began walking towards the front door, stopping to turn only once he'd coaxed the catch on the door to open. And that's when he saw me. Our eyes met – separated by understanding as much as physical distance and I gazed at him with the sum of all my sadness and confusion while he glanced back at me with a deep expression I was too young to decode. Had I made him mad? Had I done something wrong? Was that why he wanted to get away from me so badly?

"Luke...I..." he uttered eventually.

But I couldn't look at him any longer and turned to retreat back up the stairs to my room. Evidently Grandma and Grandpa hadn't been far behind Dad as the argument continued at the foot of the stairs – with Grandpa arguing with Dad over upsetting me while Grandma Irene came rushing up to my room and comforted me as I continued crying. I didn't understand any of it. And the more I didn't understand, the more tears crept out from behind my eyes.

I've never forgotten that night, no matter how much I've wanted to; and it haunted me ever since – the night Dad nearly left forever.

Chapter Three

It was unbelievable – I'd spent years thinking of this moment and all the things I'd ask and say to my parents and now they were here standing in front of me and I was speechless. I was overwhelmed – Mum had always been some mythic figure confined to a handful of photographs that still survived in 2010 and yet now she was only a couple of feet or so away from me in the flesh – living; breathing; smiling. *That* was my Mum – the one I'd never known but for vague second-hand references. Finally she was real. She was here.

Angie was slim and looked to be in her mid-twenties. From her short, Eighties "power" hairstyle along with the baggy top that drooped over one shoulder whilst being hemmed in by a complimentary belt and accented by equally as striking earrings, it was perhaps easier to notice the time I was in than it had been before. Curiously, I noticed that Angie had a warm olive glow to her skin complexion – almost Mediterranean which got me thinking about who she was – I'd never known enough about her to ever have a firm idea of where she was from.

By comparison Dad seemed fairly ordinary – slim although more muscular than Angie, dressed in worn black jeans and a faded white t-shirt depicting a band I hadn't heard of before. But by far the most easily recognisable characteristic of Dad was his glasses which looked very much like the same pair he still possessed in back in 2010 – oval in shape with a thin metallic rim keeping the lenses firmly in place.

Having invited them in Auntie Linda set about introducing me to them as, from their expressions, they clearly didn't have a clue who I was.

"Luke, this is my brother – James."

"Yeah, we've met." I replied, reaching out to shake Dad's outstretched hand formally.

It was then that irony hit me like a sobering slap as here I was shaking hands with my Dad - the most physical contact we'd shared in years and yet I was *still* a stranger to him. Unbelievable.

"We have?" he smiled curiously, "Funny, I...don't remember."

"Story of my life." I remarked candidly under my breath.

"And this is Angie..." Linda said, moving the awkward moment along.

As Angie smiled at me I became confused at what to say or feel on the matter. In my heart I wanted to call her 'Mum' and for her to make all of those years without her right with a hug and a few warm words, but in my head I knew that my doing that would only serve to seriously derail whatever was going on.

"Hello Luke. It's nice to meet you."

"It is?" I uttered as my heart longingly skipped a beat.

I'd longed to hear her say something like that for so long – to hear that she wasn't disappointed in any way by who I was. And even though I knew that she hadn't intended those words as deeply as I was interpreting them, they still warmed me with their pseudo-loving embrace.

"Likewise." I replied eventually.

Suddenly I couldn't help myself – in an instant all restraint flew right out the window and before I knew where I was I'd reached out and put my arms around her – savouring every fleeting yet glorious second.

"It's great to see you." I said, not caring how weird I appeared.

It was plain to see that everyone including Angie was taken slightly aback and it took a few seconds for her to briefly put her arms around me in response before gradually pulling away.

"Well," she said afterwards, "that's quite a welcome."

"And *this* is little Luke." Auntie Linda announced finally.

Crouching down, Linda then began playing with him…me…the *other* me, oh this was getting confusing. I stood in chilling amazement at the cheerful and lively baby in the carrier seat – that was me – not even a year old and blissfully oblivious to the upcoming events that had changed this type of picturesque family scene into the childhood I had lived through. And as I looked deeper into those glistening, innocent eyes I became ferociously resolute that I was going to ensure that *that* Luke Hudson had the childhood I never had. *This* time round, time and circumstance were going to succumb to *my* will instead of the other way around.

I must have spent ages just sitting in that living room with the others as they talked amongst themselves – just watching and listening to my parents – taking intricate note of every word and characteristic they exhibited – and finding, to my surprise, aspects of my own mannerisms echoed in how they spoke and acted. It was incredible, totally mind-blowing and such a buzz it was almost incomprehensible to take it all in. I lovingly absorbed every word they uttered and watched on as they interacted with baby Luke – bouncing him on their knees and playing peek-a-boo while continuing the conversation. And most curious of all was the detached sense of familiarity I felt when I observed baby Luke playing with a small, colourful soft ball that played a jingle whenever it was shook. It was obvious from the way my parents interacted with him, especially Dad, that I had been loved dearly – so what had happened that changed so much so permanently? It just didn't make sense. Looking at this scene in front of me now it was hard to imagine anything that bad ever happening to this young family unit and if I hadn't of lived through it firsthand I wouldn't have believed it myself.

This was all so overwhelming and yet so spectacular at the same time. I had spent so long growing up just wishing to see my parents together – to understand them and be close to them and now they were here – both sitting in the same room as me and yet equally as distant in other respects. It was, as I'd felt earlier – the height of irony. Throughout it all it was so hard not to just blurt out who I truly was but I knew that doing so would only estrange me further from them and in so doing, eliminate any feasible chance I had of altering things for the better. It was all so...ironic – the fact that I had to be a virtual stranger in order to get to know my own parents – how screwed up is that?! Time and circumstance sure had a warped sense of humour, still – I had to make the best of things, despite constantly feeling the need to play 'catch-up' with what was...and had been going on.

"So where did you two meet?" I asked, finally summoning the courage to engage my parents in conversation.

"Well I was at college doing a secretarial course and James worked in a pub just up the road. A group of us would always go there for a few hours every afternoon when we'd have a break and I took pity on this one." Angie reminisced.

"That's not the way I remember it." James retorted – looking suggestively at Angie.

"Well you must be remembering it wrong." she replied, returning the suggestive glance.

"So you're a secretary then?" I chimed-in, probing for more of an insight into who Mum was.

"Yes. At the moment, anyway. But I really want to get into business management. There's a whole world out there, Luke, and I don't want to spend mine in just one place."

"Yeah," I replied meekly, in awe.

From listening to her it was clear that Angie was passionate about making the most of herself and forging a successful career to enjoy. She clearly had ambition and the passion to realise her talent and seemed so focused – so determined that I couldn't help but admire her for that. From seeing how Dad had ended up back in 2010 – floating unhappily from job to job and being stuck in the same rut – Mum's confidence and zeal was a breath of fresh air – if only it had rubbed off on Dad as well – he might have been a different person in the future.

"How about you?" I said turning to James.

"I'm doing office work at the moment but I wanna go into graphic design. I love design – there's something about creating something artistic from scratch that's just so…amazing, you know."

It was both strange and refreshing to see this passionate sense of confidence and life in Dad. Back where I'd come from he'd hardly ever talk about his dreams or what he wanted from life – as though his life was continually on pause – waiting for some unseen element to click into place. From what little I'd seen of his sketches and random doodles over the years I knew that he possessed an innate talent when it came to the visual arts but he'd never moulded that raw talent into something constructive. Quite often back where I came from, it seemed like Dad was merely living in accordance to a basic survival philosophy – doing and earning just enough to sustain himself and, for all his faults, me – offering a regular slice of his wages to Grandma and Grandpa to cover any costs they'd accrue because of me. It wasn't like he resented me, far from it – he always seemed pleased whenever he'd see me but there was always a notable sadness that lurked in the depths of his eyes – a sadness of some unspoken origin that forced him to always keep a certain emotional distance from me. Whenever I thought about it, it was always hard labelling my feelings for Dad – part of me was so angry that he hadn't been as close as I'd wanted him to be and yet the other part of me noticed that sadness in him and wanted to reach out to him. He wasn't perfect, nobody is, but he *was* my Dad and despite his detachment I still felt a strong attachment to him.

"So why 'Luke'?" I asked, moving the conversation on.

Angie fell silent and turned to James who momentarily stopped bouncing baby Luke on his knee. A warm smile flashed across his face as his eyes closed briefly in silent reminiscence and it was both strange and fantastic to see his face encapsulate so much life where normally there was only sadness.

"After my brother." He announced.

I've got to admit – of all the potential responses I'd neither expected nor braced myself for *that* one. Did Dad even *have* a brother? Grandma and Grandpa had never spoken of another son – in fact they had barely mentioned Auntie Linda around me. In the wake of James' confusing reply I began to wonder whether I actually knew *anything* substantial about my family at all.

"Your...since when have *you* had a brother? When the hell did *this* happen?"

There were few things in life people could fully know or rely upon but family was one of them and the more all this dwelt on my mind the more it hurt – cutting deeper than any physical wound would allow.

Now it was James' turn to fall silent as Auntie Linda tried to revive the happier atmosphere.

"Maybe we should talk about something else." She suggested with an uneasy smile.

"But I..."

But it was no use. My protests fell upon deaf ears and I quickly became aware that the conversation, along with my hopes of getting an explanation from James, was about as dead as the dinosaurs. And just like the dinosaurs it seemed James' revelation was in every way a sleeping giant lost to time – at least for the moment anyway.

"Luke it's getting late. You've got school in the morning. Why don't you go get ready for bed, eh?" Linda replied.

From her tone it was clear that had been a polite invitation to leave the room. I didn't understand what I had said that had been so wrong – other than to question an obviously taboo subject – leading me to wonder whether I could manage to uncover what had been, is and will be, in time to change things for the better. More to the point – *could* I even change things?

Having no other option, I went upstairs as Linda suggested and ended up lying in a contemplative heap on the bed processing all I'd seen and heard tonight about my parents. I'd met Mum – after all this time - it was like a dream I never wanted to wake up from - she was real – I'd spoken to her. I had an uncle who I shared my name with and yet, strangest of all was the difference in Dad who appeared a complete polar-opposite to the one I'd (sort of) known back in 2010. *This* James Hudson doted unashamedly on his son and was both fully-engaged and spellbound at being a father and even with my unique foreknowledge I couldn't imagine *that* James Hudson turning into the one I'd grown up with (or without, depending on your perspective).

Next morning my head was still racing a hundred miles a minute with everything that had happened last night. Angie...I mean *Mum*...was every bit as I imagined her to be – witty, infectiously cheerful and a radiant presence that I wish had been there for me when I'd been growing up. And as for Dad – you'd be hard-pressed to polarise their personalities circa 1990 and 2010 if you tried – they were like different people – or rather very different interpretations of the same person. It was odd, *very* odd but very true. All the while I kept pondering how better things would have been if I'd of had the 1990 James Hudson around when I was younger.

Still, life in 1990 refused to stay still and I soon found myself surrounded by the sights and sounds of Lincoln Road High School and still surprised as ever at the lack of gadgetry that had been around when I'd been at high school. No mobile phones chirping away throughout the playgrounds and corridors – no flat-screen TVs or computer screens churning out up-to-the-minute news and information – no handheld games consoles that were smaller than a small brick – just people going about their everyday lives. It was serene in a way – to be immersed in an environment unblemished by the convenience of modern-day technology – of a world where people actually talked to each other instead of constantly refreshing status updates or checking text messages. It was so easy to be romanced by the different pace of life and in that sense; I think I'd fallen head over heels.

But the temporal romance wasn't exactly without its heartache.

I'd been walking to second period – around the paved pathways that connected the subsidiary buildings and prefabricated huts just off the sports field when I heard a familiar voice protest in distress nearby...

"Hey, c'mon...leave me alone...cut it out."

It was Josh – cornered and outnumbered against a wall like a hunted animal.

"What's the matter Porter? You gonna cry?"

Peering round the corner of one of the huts I saw a stocky boy, flanked by two skinnier sidekicks, giving Josh a hard time. Josh wasn't a wimp by any means but even without the mismatched ratio of him to them, they genuinely *did* seem threatening.

"Just leave me alone." Josh protested defiantly.

One of the sidekicks – the one with gelled-down jet-black hair – mimicked Josh's plea while his friends laughed. Even though I hadn't known Josh for very long I *did* know that he was family and I couldn't just stand idly by while someone that close to me was in trouble so, emerging from the corner I'd been observing from, I readied myself for a fight as I evened up the odds a bit.

"You know for a minute there it sounded like he asked you to leave him alone." I announced, making my presence known.

Turning away from Josh, the three bullies looked towards me with scowling contempt.

"Who are you?"

"Someone that doesn't appreciate people like *you* giving people like *him* a hard time."

"Oh yeah, what' you gonna do about it then?" the lead bully goaded.

"Why don't 'cha come and find out."

He stared for a couple of seconds before lunging at me in an ambitious pre-emptive strike and even though I braced myself as best I could, the impact sent the pair of us launching towards the nearby wall as we each scuffled relentlessly to gain the upper hand. It took a moment for my back to stop throbbing after absorbing the brunt of being driven into the wall but somehow I managed to hold my own. Inside I could feel the adrenaline coursing through me like an unstoppable tidal wave. It was electric. It was primal; and it felt so good to let the anger radiate out of me – almost cleansing, in a way. In that moment the bully wasn't just a guy who'd been giving Josh a hard time – he was a personification of everything my heart and mind silently raged at. As we grappled I saw him as the reason I never knew Mum...the reason Dad was so distant and detached...and the reason I felt cheated out of an existence most people take for granted. Every blow I managed to deal was a targeted counter-strike against everything I was angry at – to show that I could and indeed *would* keep on fighting – no matter who or what stood against me.

Time seemed to pass at a different rate to normal as the fight rumbled on and we kept on pushing, shoving, punching and hating until a booming voice blanketed our schoolyard battlefield like a foghorn...

"You two! Stop right there!" came the unmistakable voice of Mr Carson.

Without a second thought I panicked and, seizing the momentary advantage, punched the stocky bully in the side of the face before pushing him into his sidekicks and making a break for it. I didn't know where I was running to but I just kept going – not once daring to look back. Stopping briefly behind the art block, I studied my hands as if gazing upon foreign objects while quickly catching my breath. They had been the instrument of my fury – singing a heart's twisted song to a person equally as deserving as such contempt.

"What have you done?" I thought regretfully as the adrenaline subsided and left only logic and reason.

It did this. It always did this and I didn't like it. The anger inside was like a caged animal that roared and beat against the cage until a crack formed and them – BAM – it took over – making me explode in a fit of primal, animal rage. It always managed to get the better of me and I hated it. For years I'd described it as separate to me but certainly in the last few years I'd had to reluctantly admit that it was in fact a part of me – and one which I was resigned to deal with no matter how unprepared I was. It was just like before – just like *all* those times before. Times where that caged animal had momentarily escaped the confines of its containment and proved to be the only outlet for what I thought and felt deep down. In that split second I pictured Grandma Irene looking disappointed as she had been whenever she had been called to the school following one of these outbursts. *'Oh Luke'* she'd sigh. She'd never be angry at me – just sad; I guess because she kind of understood why I felt so messed-up. It was seeing and hearing that sadness – that disappointment in her that hurt more than any physical wounds ever could and sure enough she was saying it again – now, in my mind, as I forcibly swept a tear that'd been forming in one eye.

I set off again. This time looking for a suitable place to hide and lay low until Carson gave up looking for me. Damn – he'd looked pissed – all red-faced and authoritarian. Heaven knows I didn't want to be messing with him while he was in that mood that's for sure. I knew deep down that running from him was futile – he'd seen me after all, and sooner or later he or Mrs Burridge would find me and yank my collar for it but I just wanted some time. Time to push my inner animal back into its cage and calm down – to think without the anger clouding my perception of everything and everyone around me.

Ducking under classroom windows and round corners like some desperate secret agent I eventually found myself in a secluded area just outside the library fire exit – with loosely maintained evergreen plant life and shrubbery obscuring the view from the hut opposite.

"Hello stranger."

Startled, I span round and saw Charlotte smiling at me. I sighed with relief as my racing heartbeat began returning to normal. After the last few minutes it was good to see a friendly face.

"Charlotte? What are you doing here?"

"Getting some peace and quiet. How about you?"

"I kinda got into a scuffle with this guy that was giving Josh grief."

"And..." she smiled, sensing there was more to the story.

"And...Carson saw me."

"Oh...'fugitive' huh? Scandalous!"

"What's *your* excuse?"

"Who says I need one?" she smiled wryly.

"You don't seem the type to bunk off."

It was then that her smile faded as it became clear that something was troubling her. Granted, I hadn't known Charlotte long but I could recognise the pain hiding behind her eyes.

"I've just got some stuff going on, that's all. I'll be alright in a bit." She replied evasively.

"Anything you wanna talk about?"

I wanted to help Charlotte through whatever she was going through, although I didn't know why I felt as strongly about her as I did. It wasn't a romantic attraction but there was something vaguely familiar in the expression her eyes carried – a look I'd seen in my own reflection – a definite melancholy buried just deep enough beneath the surface to stay hidden to most while still being shallow enough to be recognisable to someone like me who knew the meaning of that look and the pain it fosters. Something *was* troubling

Charlotte; Something *big*. Her melancholic expression and vacant gaze screamed that she wanted to open up to someone and yet her lips still refused to surrender their secret pain.

"I...have to do something. Something important. But I'm not sure *how* or even *if* it'd make any difference and I only get one chance to get it right."

Whatever it was it was eating her up inside – the gravity of her sunken tone made that crystal clear. In the next few seconds where neither of us knew what to say, a few rogue tears rolled down her cheek – forcing Charlotte to wipe them away as confidently as she could.

"It's nothing, Luke. Don't worry. I'm just over-reacting."

"It doesn't sound like nothing. Maybe I can help?"

She chuckled lightly as if privately amused by what I had said. It wasn't a cruel laugh or a put-down but merely one that once again seemed to separate the two of us. She was so guarded – as if there were an invisible wall protecting her from the outside world – a wall which I couldn't seem to penetrate right now. Either way Charlotte read the confused expression that was painted on my face and adopted a sympathetic response – platonically laying a smooth hand on one side of my face and letting it gently slip away as words began escaping from her lips.

"That's sweet, Luke. Honestly. I wish I could tell you – you seem different somehow...no offence."

"None taken."

"...I don't know, it's like I only just met you yesterday..." she said thoughtfully.

Now it was my turn to chuckle lightly.

"But you *did* only meet me yesterday." I replied, slightly confused.

Charlotte looked at me as if primed to respond but fell short of actually saying anything before she thought better of it.

"Yeah, I...never mind. My head's everywhere at the minute and..."

If the sudden stop hadn't told me that something else was wrong then the look in her eyes certainly did. It was the type of look you'd expect a hunted animal to adopt when it comes face-to-face with its hunter in those precious last seconds.

"What?"

"*Busted.*" She offered under her breath while motioning behind me with her eyes.

Turning, I was confronted by the firm, stern gaze of Mr Carson. A chill tingled furiously down my spine as I instinctually looked for an exit – only to learn that I was out of luck this time. There was nowhere to run. The hunter had caught his prey. *This* time I couldn't run – I had to face up to what I had done and take control of my actions.

"*Mister* Hudson." Carson offered disarmingly.

"Mr Carson. I'm...err..."

"...in it deep and still sinking," he finished before looking at Charlotte, "And as for you...count yourself lucky I've got my hands full with *this* one. Go on – on your way before I change my mind."

Charlotte nodded, offering me another sympathetic glance before quickly making a break for her next lesson – leaving me at the mercy of Mr Carson. Beckoning me to follow him with a few flicks of his index finger Carson led me through the network of corridors, pathways and stairs in between where he'd found me and his empty classroom. He waved me inside before closing the old wooden door with the dulled brass knob and walked across to sit at his desk while I occupied one of the nearby tables in the front row.

Carson looked at me for a few seconds while considering the situation – leaving me to aimlessly ponder the potential ways this could play out – would it be good cop? Bad cop? Maybe a little of both? Yet another fine mess my anger had gotten me into.

"So...do you want to explain what that little incident with Gary Collins was all about?"

"Would it make a difference?" I replied absently, expecting a lecture either way.

"It might."

Carson's willingness to give me a fair hearing, as refreshing as it was, startled me. Was this a ruse or was he being sincere? Before at school (and by that I mean before I came to 1990) I had endured many instances where I hadn't been listened to – expected, instead, to blindly conform without further discussion or consideration of how *I* thought and felt. But Carson seemed different – he was mediating where others had dictated and listened where others had heard only their own voice and so for that reason I felt compelled to offer him the explanation he had asked for.

"Collins and his buddies were hurting someone who means something to me and I couldn't just stand by and watch it happen."

"Josh Porter?"

"Yeah. I didn't mean to get into a fight but my temper got the better of me. I just get so angry."

It was only as I said this aloud that I realised how close I'd become to Josh, Linda and Henry. Despite not knowing them long they *were* family and they cared about me; and after all this time it was warmly intoxicating to feel a part of an average nuclear family instead of a remnant from a broken home.

Carson nodded appreciatively and seemed to weigh up my explanation as he considered things while reclining slightly in his old-school wooden teacher's wheely-chair. Despite our rocky start, I was rapidly developing a level of respect for Mr Carson and his take on things. He was someone to respect – and to be respectful of.

"I understand why you did what you did, and off the record I agree with you, *but* I can't turn a blind-eye to fighting."

"I guess I just acted on instinct."

"Luke – there's nothing wrong with that but it's your temper that's the problem – until you learn to control it you'll keep on finding yourself in situations like this. Something's got you wound up tighter than a drum and until you find a way to fix that your temper will continue to run wild like it does."

He was right. 100%. There wasn't one claim I could, or even *would*, contest. Truth is my temper *had* been holding me back for as long as I could remember and it was a part of myself that I hated admitting existed or even that it was a part of me.

"I know, it's just...I've been angry for so long that I don't even know *what* it is that I'm angry with anymore. It's like an animal inside of me - too vicious and primal." I confessed, feeling uneasy airing these otherwise private musings.

"Animals can be tamed Luke." Carson replied after a few seconds.

I smiled thinly. What he said made sense and the point he was driving at was crystal clear but understanding a concept and making it a reality were two very different things.

"So," I piped up, "Is this the part where you sentence the accused?"

"It *was* until we had this chat. Tell you what – come and find me after school and I'll have figured out a way for you to make good on what's happened."

I merely nodded in compliance. It was strange how Carson had come to possess such respect from me in such a short space of time but it was good to feel like there was at least someone who would give me a fair hearing.

"Right, on your way then. I've got a class to prepare for."

*   *   *

I kept my head down for the rest of the day – trying my best to counter-balance the impact my temper had left earlier on in the day. When I went back to Mr Carson's room at the end of the day he was part-way through marking a stack of books. Even though the door was open, I knocked lightly to get his attention and he turned – removing his reading glasses before addressing me.

"Ah yes, Mister Hudson, come in."

I stepped inside not knowing what would be asked of me. I was kinda nervous. It always felt like this in the aftermath of my temper – like I was walking on eggshells around everyone – a stark reminder of the Jekyll-and-Hyde split between the anger I felt and the person I knew I was inside.

"Can I ask you a question?" he asked candidly.

"Sure" I shrugged.

"Why do you think you get angry?"

"I don't know...*stuff*...it's...complicated."

"What if you could simplify the problem?"

"How d'you mean?" I asked uneasily.

"Well, all problems have solutions and from what we spoke about earlier I could see how much *this* problem troubles you. I think you need to find some clarity on why you feel that way so, with that in mind, I'd like you to write an essay about your anger – what you think causes it and how it makes you feel. Reflection is an important life skill, Luke. Come back to me when you've done it and we'll talk about it some more, okay?"

There wasn't much else I could say or do other than nod in compliance. For the first time in ages it felt like I had a chance to take the fight to my anger – to tame that wild animal inside; and I was going to give this challenge my full attention. Carson's sincerity was unmistakable – he *really* was on my side – he *really* wanted to help and so I was more than happy to meet him halfway.

Mr Carson excused me after that and as I ventured towards where Josh and Charlotte were waiting for me at the main gate, my mind began churning over all the things that feed into my anger – the things that fuel the fire that consumes all in its wake.

*   *   *

After meeting Josh and Charlotte at the main gate they led the way to a cafe they liked to hang out in. I expected a backstreet greasy spoon but was surprised to be greeted by a secluded store located in a quaint alleyway arcade just off Sutton High Street. The cafe – *"Artie's"* – was lovingly and tastefully decorated in an artistic assortment of pastel blue, yellow and pink neon lights, art-deco-esque wall-mounted light fixtures, chrome-clad stools and tables, along with a selection of arcade machines and an old-school jukebox in one corner – spill over from the 1980s. The counter was topped with white marble, adorned with several of the chrome-clad stools and tended to by a young woman who looked to be in her late twenties. Josh and Charlotte made a move for the jukebox – selecting a short playlist before hitting the arcade machines, whilst I walked over to the counter and ordered a drink.

The woman behind the counter looked over at me and smiled. I read her name badge as she wiped the freshly cleaned glasses after handing me my drink with a friendly smile – "Grace" it read. Grace had frizzy back-length chestnut hair with red streaks held together in a loose ponytail. And then, while wiping another glass, she came closer towards me.

"Cheer up – it might never happen."

"Too late – it already has." I replied glibly while absently twirling the plastic straw around in my slushie.

"Anyone would think you didn't want to be here."

"I don't!" I answered – still adrift amidst all of the thoughts that being here in 1990 had unearthed.

Little did I know that things were about to get even stranger as Grace leaned in closer and adopted a more serious tone and facial expression.

"You wanted this, Luke. Remember?"

"I don't understand. What are you talking about? And how do you know my name?"

"Your birthday wish...your 21st birthday to be exact...do you remember?" she began before perfectly mimicking my voice with spine-chilling accuracy, "...I wish I could know my parents better...I wish things were different."

Spooked to the core I recoiled slightly and shot up off the bar stool, taking a step back in shock.

"How...how do you know that? That was private...I never even said that out loud...that was twenty odd years from now."

Grace kept her serious expression fixed on me as she returned to drying glasses. I didn't know what was happening – it was all so strange – HA, yeah – like the *rest* of this made any sense. What she knew was impossible – simply impossible. There was no conceivable way Grace could know something I wished for years from now. It just wasn't possible – was it?

"Do you believe in God, Luke?"

"I don't know," I answered, puzzled, "I guess."

"Well He believes in you and He's given you a rare chance to achieve your wish, and all you can do is complain. If you *really* want to go back, I suppose I can help you with that..." she announced sharply before clapping her hands twice together.

Suddenly the cafe faded from sight until all that was left was me – alone in darkness. Somehow I could feel others close by despite not being able to see a few centimetres past my outstretched hand. It was like one of those out-of-body experiences – everything seemed familiar and yet distorted at the same time. Then, out of the darkness shrouded around me, I began hearing muffled voices that gradually became clearer as I continued staring into nothingness.

"Luke...Luke, darling, wake up. Can you hear me, sweetheart?"

It was Grandma. In an instant my heart began pounding – I'd missed her since being in 1990 and yet I couldn't see her. Where was she? It was as if all my pent-up emotions had come flooding out at once – desperation, panic, loss, anxiety.

"Grandma...I'm here. I can hear you. Grandma..."

Then came Grandpa.

"Would you lot stop gawping and phone a bloody ambulance?!"

He sounded scared. I'd never heard him *that* scared before. Was I still in the restaurant – merely unconscious on the floor? Had I been there this whole time? These past few days – had they been mere seconds in reality? What was going on? I didn't understand.

Suddenly I felt pressure on my chest – as though a first aider or paramedic were trying to revive me. I thought about waking up back in 2010 – back to familiar surroundings and people I knew but then something came over me - a thought...no, more like a realisation of what I'd be giving up if I went back now. I had been given an opportunity to achieve what I had wished for and, looking back on it now, Grace had been right – all I did in response was complain. Regret coursed through me as the realisation that my blind anger had spoilt what should have been a once-in-a-lifetime opportunity and so, fighting against the revival attempts, I turned and called out to the only person who could help me now.

"Grace... I'm sorry. Grace...are you there? Can you hear me? I'm sorry. It's just so overwhelming – I didn't mean to sound ungrateful. I didn't understand why I was there. Please, give me another chance. Grace..."

To my utter relief Grace appeared instantly in front of me, smiling and bathed in a warm glowing aura of golden light. Who was she? In fact, for now, scratch that – it didn't matter as long as she could help.

"I'm sorry that this was so painful for you but you needed to understand the magnitude of the chance you've been given. Not everyone gets this opportunity."

"I understand," I said, clasping my hands together in desperation, "Just please...*don't* send me back. Not now – not like this."

Grace considered things silently for a moment before smiling and once again clapping her hands together twice. Within a flash we were back in the cafe – in 1990. It was as if no time had passed at all – I was still sat at the counter with my slushie in front of me and Grace was still drying glasses.

Looking around briefly I saw Josh and Charlotte still playing on the arcade machines over in the corner while the jukebox continued to play the songs they had chosen. They were blissfully unaware that anything had happened. It was as if Grace and I hadn't gone anywhere and only the pair of us knew any different. I turned back to Grace who offered a friendly smile and a wink.

"Thank you," I uttered eventually, "I appreciate it."

"Only time will tell, now, won't it? Just make the most of it Luke."

"Can I really change things then?"

"Well, 'yes' and 'no'. Some things can be changed, others can't. The difficult bit is working out which is which. What I *can* tell you is that there *are* things here in your personal history that can be altered for the better but you'll have to find out those bits for yourself. And be careful – this is a rare case."

"Why? How?"

"Because it intersects with someone else's destiny. It's rare that two such cases are linked like this and it complicates things somewhat but...I'm sure you'll discover what I'm talking about in your own time."

"Grace, how do you know all this?"

"It's my job to know."

"Your job?" I echoed, motioning around the cafe.

"What kind of Angel of Destiny would I be if I didn't know a stitch about people, hmm?"

"Angel of Destiny?!" I repeated, bemused, "*You're* the Angel of Destiny?"

"No, I'm *an* Angel of Destiny. There aren't enough of us to offer a one-to-one service nowadays so we work by a caseload basis and surprise, surprise – your case was assigned to me."

I laughed. With everything else having seemed too strange it was perplexingly amusing that *this* almost made perfect sense. It was *so* odd and yet *so* plausible. I'd grown up in a family where religion and spirituality was important. I *did* believe – truly. I just didn't expect God to be so hands-on. Grace was right – I had been given a unique and wonderful chance and I wasn't going to let it pass me by anymore.

"Caseload basis?! You make Heaven sound like a business."

"Everything needs structure, Luke. Heaven's no different."

"I...see."

I didn't really but there wasn't much else to say. What else *could* you say when the...I mean, *an* Angel of Destiny presents themselves to you? And I thought waking up in 1990 was weird.

"Now then – I'll be here to offer you any guidance or support you might need but remember – you must be responsible for your own destiny, okay?"

"I understand."

By the time we left *Artie's* sometime later I'd already reflected on the chance I'd been given and how I could turn things around. It was overwhelming to think that I could change things that had gone wrong in the past – I had the opportunity to fix my family before it fragmented beyond repair. I wasn't going to squander this chance – I was going to make the most out of it – even if it did mean coping with another place in time and all the associated weirdness.

Chapter Four

Back at Linda's, which (by the way) was fast feeling like home, I made a start on thinking up ideas for the reflective essay Mr Carson had set me. Perhaps in writing I could say that which my lips could not. Who knows? In any event, I was determined to give it a damn good try.

It was a fairly grey and grizzly afternoon – with swollen clouds looming ominously over the neighbourhood but even that didn't deter my renewed sense of vigour; after speaking with Grace earlier I was keen to show both how grateful I was for the chance and how keen I was to make the most of it – and that meant fitting in and learning to control my temper instead of the other way round.

I must have had a major epiphany as by the time I heard a knock at my bedroom door some time later, I had already penned a page and a half of the essay – finding mostly that the words virtually wrote themselves the more I got into it. Looking up from the small collection of lined paper I saw Uncle Henry standing in the doorway – still dressed in his work attire – minus the tie.

"Hey," I smiled softly.

"Hi. Have you got a moment?"

"Sure." I replied, pushing my rucksack off the bed.

Uncle Henry came in and sat nearby on the edge of the bed where my rucksack had been. He looked serious yet unimposing as he posed himself to speak.

"I...heard about the fight."

"Oh," I sighed, expecting the mother – or rather the *father* of all lectures.

But to my surprise Uncle Henry never raised his tone – nor did he show any signs of imminently exploding with anger.

"Why did you get into a fight?" he asked calmly.

"Some boys where giving Josh a hard time. Josh is family and family stick together. At least they're supposed to, anyway. I'm sorry if it offended you but I just couldn't stand by and watch someone I care about get hurt."

I meant every word of what I said. It was strange because up until now I'd been so consumed with being in a different time that I hadn't properly acknowledged the family I had been introduced to as a result of being here. I was more than grateful for being introduced to them, and for being taken in by them and really wanted, more than anything, to get to know them better – to discover my roots; not to mention why there had been no earthly trace of them in the future I'd come from. Just knowing I had more family out there made me feel good – like I was from somewhere – like I belonged.

"I understand why you did it and I think your motives are admirable. Family *should* stick together. But violence isn't the solution to problems – more often it's the cause of them..."

I was about to interject but Uncle Henry motioned for me to keep listening.

"...But I guess you've already been put through the mill about all this."

"Yeah once or twice." I answered casually, briefly remembering similar instances from childhood.

"Well if you'd do me a favour I'd be more than happy to say no more about it."

"What kind of favour?"

"Babysitting – tonight?"

"I'd of thought Josh could have occupied himself." I laughed.

"Not Josh!" Henry replied, cracking a smile, "Your Aunt and I are going out to dinner with James and Angie tonight and their babysitter cancelled at the last minute."

The details of what Henry had said suddenly slapped me in the face like the bitter chill on a winter's day. "James and Angie". He was talking about my parents which meant...I'd be babysitting myself – my *younger* self to be exact. It was wrong on so many levels but what else could I do? Man, this just got weirder and weirder.

"So what d'you say? Will you do it? I'll take you there and bring you back afterwards."

I stumbled over what to say for a moment until feeling brave enough to kerb the spine-tingling weirdness long enough to mount a coherent response.

"Sure...sure...I'll do it."

"Great. Thanks Luke. HA! How odd – you've both got the same name. How about that?" he said before getting up and leaving the room.

"You have *no* idea!" I muttered under my breath.

*   *   *

Uncle Henry drove me to James and Angie's flat around 8pm and for the entire journey I sat perplexed in the passenger seat as the dynamics of what was about to happen still seemed too bizarre to take in. I was going to be babysitting myself – it was the stuff of crazy dreams and yet it was happening. Growing up I'd seen a handful of films and TV series that touched upon so-called "temporal mechanics". Each had its own unique theoretical standpoint on what could and would happen when someone came into physical contact with themselves from another time leading me to ponder what the outcome of tonight would be – would interacting with my younger self pre-empt a collapse of the timeline or force me out of existence? "Same matter occupying the same point in space/time" and all of that complicated scientific stuff .Surely Grace would have warned me if I were in any danger. After all, she *had* said that there were rules to being here – and limitations to what I could and could not do but still, she wouldn't let me walk blindly into danger. Resolutely I opted to kerb my anxiety-fuelled paranoia and began thinking of the opportunities I'd have to learn about my parents tonight instead.

When we arrived at the flat it was Dad, or rather – James, who opened the door and led us inside to the lounge. After stepping into the lounge behind Uncle Henry I stopped for a moment to take in the room – absorbing some manner of aura or indication of my parents. The room sported sleek, matching black ash furniture, two black leather sofas of different sizes and a colourful canvas baby seat – complete with baby.

I became mesmerized by the sight of my younger self as James and Henry talked between themselves. It was incredible to think that that baby was me – we were the same person and yet we were both here at the same time. This *was* the stuff of dreams – purely mind-blowing in the most surreal and exhilarating of ways imaginable. Looking into those tiny eyes I noticed a twinkle of innocence that I'd never seen in *my* reflection before. It was hard to stomach knowing what would change that smiling, playful baby into me and it was precisely that privileged knowledge that rallied my confidence and determination at what I had to do – at what I *had* to change for the better. In that instant I was adamant that that innocent baby in front of me would never be hurt like I had. He wouldn't turn into me. I'd make damn sure of that.

"Angie...you ready yet?" James called into the hallway.

"Nearly - just a second." came the disembodied reply.

That was another thing. James was so alive here in 1990 so much so that it was difficult to reconcile the fact he and the James Hudson I knew were the same person. They were so polarised from each other. He was happy here and needed no encouragement to interact with my younger self. I watched, entranced, as James played peek-a-boo with his son and regretted not having been able to remember moments like this. *This* James Hudson had no reservations with being close to his son – to me – or showing how he felt and it was a tear-jerking moment to acknowledge that Dad really *did* care about me. I really *did* mean something to him – even though my version of him had problems communicating that. He was my Dad and for the first time in a long time I didn't mind admitting it to myself. I was James Hudson's son and that felt good.

"Thanks for doing this at such short notice." James said, turning to me after finishing playing peek-a-boo.

"It's no problem. You're welcome."

Just then, baby Luke started grizzling while flapping his arms up at James, leading the latter to scoop the other me up and gently rock him in his arms while pacing around in a squashed sort of circular motion.

"There, there. It's okay. Daddy's here. There we are...good boy." James soothed.

It was amazing just how fatherly James was and how in-tune he was with baby Luke. I felt bad for how I'd misjudged *my* James Hudson about not caring. Evidently something major had happened around this time that had derailed this otherwise idyllic family unit.

Angie eventually floated into view — noticeably dressed to impress with a scarlet evening dress — complete with shoulder-pads and a small, sleek black handbag lovingly perched upon her shoulder. I was just as awe-struck with her as I had been the other day — it was great to finally be around the mother I'd been without for so long. She was the missing part of my roots and now as I met her for the second time I began accepting her as a person as opposed to some detached mythologized ideal. As she stepped into the doorway I began to smell a hint of her perfume on the breeze — some fruity, summery fragrance that was almost as captivating as her smile. *That* was Angie — *that* was my Mum.

"You look...great." I said.

It was hard fighting the urge to let my guard down and tell her everything in the vain (and somewhat naive) hope that she would make everything alright. I wanted to tell her and James who I was — I wanted them to look upon me in the same way James had with my younger counterpart. But inside I knew it was a foolish idea — more sentiment than sense and so, regretfully, I struggled to continue being slightly detached from the pair of them.

"Thank you Luke, that's really sweet." She smiled, fiddling with one of her earrings.

"We should probably get going." remarked Henry after consulting his watch.

"OK, well he should be alright," James said, "I'll put him to bed now. He shouldn't be any trouble – little fella's usually really good – aren't you? Yes you are...yes you are. Just be sure to check on him every twenty minutes or so."

"Don't worry – he'll be fine while I'm here."

James carried off baby Luke after that as Angie finished rummaging through her handbag and turned her attention to me again.

"There's drinks and snacks in the kitchen so feel free to help yourself. I left the number for the restaurant on the fridge in case you need to get hold of us in an emergency. We shouldn't be back too late. Thanks again for doing this; you wouldn't believe the last time I got to do this."

Angie's tone was laced with the impression that she felt confined somehow and I guess I could understand why – the added responsibility of having a baby must seem overwhelming at first – new rules to live by and new things to learn on the go – perhaps Angie was just finding the adjustment to parenthood tough to get to grips with. Was *this* what had driven her away? Had *I* driven her away? Either way I couldn't help but feel sorry for her and found myself fighting that familiar urge to reach out and tell her everything and for her to make everything right. I wanted to reassure her that everything would be alright this time round – that I'd make sure of it. But for all my optimism the thought of telling her everything and then being rejected as crazy kept my secret firmly bottled up inside. There was too much at stake for me to risk not being close to my parents now – I *needed* to be close to them if I was to stand even a fighting chance of making things right.

After everyone left I sat in the living room and contemplated how I could turn things in 1990 around for the better. I was working on hunches and instincts but I couldn't let that stop me. There had to be something I could and *would* do. My thoughts soon trailed to my parents and before long I found myself pacing about the flat – looking at all of the photos and artefacts of my parents and their lives as if looking around some personal museum. All around the flat were snapshots that charted Mum and Dad's relationship: comical poses from a summertime holiday on a golden beach – they looked so young – around my age maybe, perhaps a little younger; the pair of them dancing at a wedding reception – looking blissfully in love. Still, it couldn't have been *their* wedding though – neither of them looked the part of bride and groom and, to my knowledge, they had never married; Next was a photo of them embracing while sharing a Christmas kiss – with Angie's head curled up on James' shoulder. Both were wearing knitwear that looked extremely dated – in fact, Angie's top even sported some killer shoulder-pads and an abnormally large frizzy perm – total Eighties excess! Then there was a photo of James sitting at Angie's bedside holding a familiar newborn baby in the hospital; and finally – there was one of James sitting on the sofa in the living room strumming away enthusiastically on his acoustic guitar as the little baby next to him looked on curiously.

It was so strange - they were my parents and yet I still felt like an outsider rummaging through something private and off-limits. When my tour of my parents flat reached its natural conclusion I went to check on baby Luke – being careful not to wake him...me up. Again – strange, I know. Along the way I cautiously ventured into my parents bedroom. My tour hadn't taken me in here – I'd been too nervous to enter their room before now but finally my curiosity and desire for knowledge about them forced me inside.

James and Angie's room was slightly messy – a kind of organised "lived-in" kind of mess – with small stacks of laundry on top of the dresser and a small assortment of boxes from baby-related items stacked haphazardly in one corner. It was easy to tell who's side of the bed was who's – with Dad's acoustic guitar resting against a bedside table that contained a worn paperback completed with makeshift receipt bookmark, a Union-flag guitar pick, a half-empty tumbler of water and his glasses case whereas Mum's side of the bed was furnished with another beside table that contained a small trinket box that housed some smaller items of jewellery, an opaque sky-blue bottle of perfume and a small bedside lamp that matched neither the bedding nor the wallpaper. I sprayed a small amount of Mum's perfume in the air and became immersed with my framing of her in connection to that scent. Closing my eyes, I began seeing a slideshow of imagined childhood memories surrounding me and Angie before the fragrant aroma dissipated and my eyes awoke to the stark reality of being a stranger in my parent's room once again.

It all seemed so basic in theory – I wanted *them...us...*for the three of us to be a family and yet the reality (at least the one I came from) couldn't have been any further from that ideal. Why had I been denied that? It wasn't fair and hopefully, God willing, it was also changeable. The potent wave of romanticised idealism washed over me once again until I became engulfed in imagined scenarios of family life with Mum and Dad – it all seemed so plausible if only I could keep my family together. Those feelings were intoxicating and some of the warmest I ever remember feeling despite being mere flights of fantasy at the moment; but for those few precious, timeless seconds they were as real and near-tangible as anything I *could* remember.

Sobering from the intoxicating illusions I realised that I was probably overdue to check in on *baby* Luke. Even though making that distinction in my mind, it was still mind-blowing to know that we were the same person – just years apart.

Entering his little room at the rear of the flat felt odd and out of place in the same way my parent's room had. I just couldn't shake the feeling that I was intruding somehow – like I was somewhere I wasn't supposed to be. Perhaps it was my mind's way of coping with being in a different time – some sort of perceived temporal awareness but either way it was weird enough to send a chilling tingle travelling through my bones every time I considered it.

To my surprise there were a couple of things in the room that I actually remembered – toys that I vaguely recognised; books I remember grandma and grandpa reading to me at bedtimes when I was little – they'd always do the voices; A thin smile emerged on my otherwise awe-struck face as memories of those times flashed briefly in and out of view. Finally, sitting on a shelf next to where my younger self was sleeping was a stuffed toy – a very soft blue elephant. It had been my inseparable companion as a kid. I used to take that elephant everywhere. I reached for it cautiously as if reaching for some forbidden fruit and held it close for a second while the memories and emotions this innocent stuffed toy contained came flooding back to me. It was with the greatest reluctance that I put it back upon the shelf before looking inside the crib at the sleeping visage of the person I used to be many years ago.

"I can't promise I'll make it perfect but I'm gonna do my utmost to make it better. I don't ever want you to become me – you don't deserve that, you deserve a happy childhood. I'll do what I can while I'm here but there are some things that *you* need to be ready for. There are people out there, people that want to change you – to mould you into some well-oiled cog. Whatever you do, don't let them win. You're your own person – with dreams and aspirations. Don't let them jade them for you like they did me. Living with that is the worst hell imaginable – next to not knowing your parents. I guess what I'm trying to say is that it'll be tough but hang in there. I don't know how long I'll be here for – or how much I'm allowed to change. Some things may be left up to you to do later on. Just do your best, that'll be enough."

He stirred gently in his sleep and flexed the tiny fingers on one hand as he shuffled his head to the left slightly. I knew he couldn't hear me or even understand what I'd been saying but it felt better to share the thoughts and feelings that usually remained chained-up inside – screaming to be heard. Besides, he deserved an explanation along with some advice from someone who had lived through what he would have to if I couldn't change certain things. He deserved better and I was determined to give him just that.

*   *   *

For the next couple of hours I sat trying to learn everything I could about my parents from what was accessible in the flat – finally cradling two photo albums I'd found in the living room cabinet for well over an hour and gazing upon the silent narrative of their lives both together and apart. In some ways it helped me feel closer to them as strange as that may seem. They were more than the limited sum of my recollection or speculation even if (paradoxically) I was just as distant from them here as I had been back home.

It was only the sound of a door key jingling in the lock that tore me out of the contemplative world I'd immersed myself in. A quick blink-and-you-miss-it glance at the clock told me it was gone half eleven and I shot up from the sofa in anticipation as the sound of clippy-cloppy formal shoes echoed almost hypnotically in the hallway before James, I mean...*Dad*, emerged in the doorway.

"Hey Luke."

After everything I'd thought of and managed to piece together tonight I wanted so much to call him Dad but, just like with Mum earlier, it would have only confused things and so I had to regretfully curb my emotions.

"Hey," I replied after a second's pause, "Where's Angie?"

"She...stayed on to meet a friend afterwards." came the uncomfortable answer before James' usual more upbeat tone kicked back in, "He wasn't too much trouble was he?"

"Nah, it was just like being here with myself." I answered wryly, aware that Dad wouldn't find the same humour in that statement that I did.

When James disappeared momentarily to check on his infant son I quickly shuffled the photo albums on the sofa back into the cabinet I'd liberated them from earlier. I hated all of the sneaking around but without freaking everyone out it was the only option I had. I had to work in the shadows, at least for now.

"He's out like a light, bless him." James said, fiddling with his cufflinks upon returning.

"He really means a lot to you, doesn't he?"

With that, James looked at me bemused as if I'd asked him the most absurd question he'd ever heard of.

"Of course he does. He's my little boy – I'm so proud of him."

I remained silent – overwhelmed by a furore of mixed emotions. I had waited all my life to hear him say that – to finally feel wanted by and connected to him. But the buried rage I'd harboured towards him all these years boiled over – if he truly meant that then why had he never been there when I had been growing up? Why had he kept himself so distant from me? I didn't know how I felt about him right now – I seemed to love him and hate him in equal measure, with a strange inner conflict enveloping me. What could I do to ensure *this* version of James Hudson is the one that's still around in 2010?

As he casually rolled up his sleeves James started humming a tune that seemed distantly yet distinctively familiar. It was the kind of tune that sweetly seduced your ears and crept inside your mind to linger for sometime afterwards. Something about it ignited fragments of dormant memories.

"That tune – what is it?" I asked.

"*Johnny and Mary,*" he answered, "It's a song that means a lot to me – one of those rare ones that really reaches out to you, you know? The words – they're so powerful and true, I relate to them a lot. I sing it to Luke actually as a kind of lullaby when he has trouble sleeping or settling down."

And then it clicked – the acoustic guitar and that tune – I *could* vaguely remember Dad strumming away on his guitar when I'd been younger. He'd moved in temporarily with Grandma and Grandpa for a few months one time when he was between flats. It was a hazy recollection – probably because I'd been so young at the time - but it was solid enough for me to believe in.

I wanted to stay and ask him more but was stopped short by James handing me a crumpled ten-pound banknote from his pocket.

"Thanks again for tonight Luke."

"I...didn't do this for money. I did it because we're family – and family are there for each other, right?"

I couldn't take his money – I didn't want it. I wanted *him* and Mum – I wanted my family – the way it was supposed to be. James, though slightly taken aback, smiled and nodded appreciatively before returning the banknote to his trouser pocket.

"That's very noble of you, Luke, thank you. I hope *my* Luke turns out like you. Anyway, Henry's waiting for you outside but I'll see you soon though, right?" he said, outstretching his hand.

Giving into my feelings, I reached forward with arms outstretched and enjoyed the first proper hug with Dad I'd had in years – savouring every second whilst knowing that this would only be a fleeting moment. James patted my back in a manly and reassuring manner before pulling away gently.

"Count on it." I smiled.

With that, James then showed me out and after he'd closed the door I leaned against the cold wooden exterior of the front door as my head and heart both yearned to be back on the other side of the door. A small window from what must have been my parent's room was ajar a few feet away and, above the nocturnal melody of nearby traffic, I could hear Dad slowly strumming the signature riff to that all-so-familiar tune – to the song that I now knew meant a great deal to him. *Now* I was resolute. *Now* I was primed.

"Don't worry Dad. I'm gonna make everything alright. I promise. No matter what, I'm gonna come through. We *will* be a family again."

March 2003 (Aged 13)

It had been an utter pig of a day. One of those days where it seems like a nuclear bomb has just gone off in your life and everything that once was stable and normal was now aimlessly flailing around in the resulting mushroom cloud. After an "eventful" day at school, I'd been summoned to the kitchen upon getting home and told to sit at the small wooden table. It was clear from the expressions on my grandparent's faces that they were both as far removed from amused as one could get. Grandma sat opposite me with a look of stone-cold authority on her face while Grandpa looked across at me while leaning back casually against the draining board with his arms folded.

"Do you want to explain what happened today?" asked Grandma eventually after a prolonged contemplative silence.

Shrugging dismissively I remained silent – opting not to share or recount what had happened. I was angry and frustrated and although none of it was aimed at Grandma and Grandpa, I just wasn't in the mood to be lectured. None of this was fair. I hated it.

"Don't shrug your shoulders at us young man, answer the question." came the fatherly tone of Grandpa.

"I lost my temper, okay. It's no big deal." I sulked, looking down at the table-top.

"Luke, you've been suspended from school. We think that is a big deal."

It was clear to notice the deep concern in Grandma's voice. At first I hated the situation that had led to this, before that same hate turned inward against me – making me hate myself for having let the situation lead me to this outcome.

I sighed. They were disappointed in me and that hurt more than anything else could. And I didn't blame them; in fact I'd be disappointed with me to if I were on their side of the table right about now. It was always the same thing. I just couldn't seem to help it. Somehow my temper always seemed to just get the better of me and end up leaving me to deal with the aftermath.

"They wanted us to do this stupid essay about our parents." I began, *"When I said I couldn't write about my parents, people laughed at me and then the teacher gave me a hard time for not writing anything and I just...lost my temper."*

"You trashed the classroom, nearly injuring some of the other people in there, and then you threw a chair through a window."

When Grandpa put it like that it made it seem like some pre-meditated monster-rampage but in reality it had been a few seconds, maximum. A few seconds where that thick, black rage stuck to me like hot tar and made me...different. I hadn't intended to hurt anyone – I just needed to release some of that pent-up anger before it exploded through my chest and consumed me whole.

"I'm sorry."

"Whatever would possess you to do something like that, Luke? That's not like you." asked Grandma.

"Because I'm sick of being reminded that my parents don't want me, okay. It hurts too much."

"Oh sweetheart, that's not true. Don't say that."

Empathy was foremost in their gaze as they considered me and the situation from the other side of the table and despite it having hurt to voice that rage just now it was fast healing — like I had needed to expel it from my system.

"It's true to me, Grandma. Dad goes from week to week without calling or even acknowledging me and as for Mum...well, who knows?! It's not fair. Why does it have to be like this? What did I do?"

At that point Grandma got up, walked round to me and wrapped her arms around me lovingly.

"Oh Luke. You didn't do anything. None of what's happened is your fault. What happened was because of your parents, not you, sweetheart. We'll speak to your Dad, okay? But you really need to control that temper of yours instead of the other way round."

"I know. I'm sorry." I sighed with genuine remorse.

"Go on — up to your room. We'll call you down when dinner's ready." Grandpa smiled reassuringly.

Chapter Five

The next day was Saturday. Finally, a day away from school which had been tough enough the first time round – back when I really *had* been fifteen except *this* time it was like being the victim of an overly drawn-out joke. But that aside I was beginning to feel attached to this place and the people around me. Don't get me wrong, I still missed Grandma and Grandpa like crazy and couldn't wait to see them again but it was refreshing to know that I had more family here – even if they didn't know who I truly was.

Yeah, actually, about that – it was still weird to get my head around but according to Grace they all knew that I *was* family but not necessarily where exactly I came from on the family tree, so to speak. To them I was a nephew of Linda although thanks to the divine intervention they'd never question where or even who from. That afternoon in the cafe Grace had chuckled so much whilst explaining things to me that I'm surprised I managed to absorb any of the details. It had all sounded so detached from reality and yet so plausible. It was all so impossible but when you'd been whisked back in time, turned into a twenty-one year old teenager (who everyone believes is fifteen) and brought face to face with an Angel of Destiny – you're pretty much ready to accept anything. I know I was.

This place, this opportunity was amazing. By now my initial displacement angst had given way to the rising sense of curiosity and awe that I felt the more I stayed here.

By the time I went downstairs for breakfast there was only Josh in the kitchen; in fact I think it was just us two in the house.

"Hey," I said, "Where is everyone?"

"It's Saturday," Josh answered before enjoying another hearty spoonful of cereal, "Mum's gone to see a friend and Dad's been sent to do the shopping so don't expect to see either of them till mid afternoon."

Reaching for the cupboard I began making a cup of coffee – I hadn't had one since I'd arrived and so the opportunity to have one now was simply too tempting to ignore.

"Didn't you want to go with them?"

"Are you kidding? This is like *the* only time I get to myself. Besides – Mum's friend has this dog that's always excited and jumps all over you; and Dad always ends up getting trolley rage."

"Fair enough." I replied, pouring the hot water into the mug and stirring the contents.

"Thanks for yesterday by the way. I...never got a chance to say it before." Josh said, adopting a less jovial tone.

The fight. With all that had happened last night I'd almost forgotten about my run-in with the school bully yesterday.

"Well, we gotta stick together, right – being family and all?"

"Yeah but, still...thanks."

He was serious. That one act of loyalty truly meant a lot to him and his appreciation, in turn, meant a lot to me. It felt so good to be a part of something bigger – to know that I had common roots and a special bond with these people; and in a way it was as if I were seeing the world anew through different eyes.

"It's cool." I replied before taking the first precious sip of coffee.

Josh and I continued talking over breakfast – discussing all manner of things – some random, some philosophical until the subject of him, Charlotte and the awkward and obvious chemistry between them came up.

"So what's the deal with you two anyway?"

"Deal? You mean like, 'are we going out'? Pfft – I wish. It's weird – we've been really close for ages and I *do* like her a *lot* but we never seem to...you know...talk about it."

It was clear just how much the conflict of interest was cutting into him – of potentially risking a great friendship by making an unsuccessful or non-mutual advance. There was little else in life worse than unrequited love – after all, *everyone* deserved *someone*.

"Perhaps you should."

Josh scoffed in mock horror – reminding me just how difficult and complicated it could be to be a teenager in love – I only had to think back to my own teenage years to get reacquainted with that maelstrom of raw emotion and desire – of childhood ideals and their often stark adulthood contrasts. Love wasn't always the stuff of storybooks or fairy tales – sometimes love could be complicated and jagged and hurt like hell, so I appreciated how Josh must be feeling.

But Josh was obviously uncomfortable with talking about it and swiftly made a play to change the subject.

"Maybe we should talk about something else – like 'what the deal is' with you and that *'Incredible Hulk'* temper of yours – you were like a different person."

He hadn't said or meant it maliciously but either way it touched upon a raw nerve – upon a part of myself I hated to acknowledge – the part of me I couldn't control.

"Everyone has a temper Josh." I replied evasively.

"I guess."

*　　*　　*

Josh had mentioned meeting Charlotte later that afternoon at Artie's Cafe and had invited me along. I didn't have much else to do so I said yes but there was something I wanted to do first. Last night had been a rush – seeing my parents (together) and being in their home – it was unreal and so intoxicating that I had to go over there again today – to see them, to talk to them, to feel connected to them; and so retracing the route Uncle Henry took in the car whilst counter-balancing my local knowledge circa 2010, I made my way over to my parents flat around late morning. In truth I didn't know what to say or do when I was there but I just had this overwhelming urge to be there. I didn't know whether it was a natural parent-child instinct or because I'd missed them for so long – perhaps it was both, either way every fibre in my being was telling me I should be there.

From the moment Angie opened the front door I could tell she was surprised to see me and it was truly uplifting to see her, although I still had to fight the urge to call her 'Mum'. She was wearing a sports sweatshirt and light blue jeans today and had her hair tied back into a bushy ponytail and yet to me she still looked just as radiant as when I'd first seen her the other day at Linda's.

"Oh, hey Luke. What a surprise. Come in."

"Thanks," I smiled shyly as I stepped through the threshold for the second time in as many days, "I'm...not interrupting am I?"

"No. I was just cleaning — Saturday's about the only time I get to do it. James has taken Luke to the shops with him so it's the perfect opportunity to get some housework done."

I followed Angie into the kitchen where she'd been wiping down the cupboards and worktops. The room had that just-clean scent of lemon along with a faint trace of bleach or detergent.

"D'you want some help?"

Angie looked at me curiously and smiled, "*You* want to help me clean the flat on a *Saturday*?! Are you 'on' something?"

Unknowingly I'd amused her and I guess it was kind of odd for a teenager to volunteer to help clean up, let alone on a weekend; but for me I'd just be glad of spending some time getting to know the mother I'd never been allowed to be close to.

"Yeah - I'm on shop-brand instant coffee but that aside, I really *would* like to help."

"Well, in that case," she said nodding towards a mop and bucket in the corner, "I'd appreciate some help with the floor. Could you do that while I tackle this cooker?"

"Sure."

And so I began helping the mother I never knew, and who (even now) didn't know me. It felt so natural to be around her — there was this instinctual feeling inside me that felt connected to her even though in most respects we were still relative strangers to one another; another reminder if any were needed of that inherent parent-child bond which was strange to acknowledge, seeing as I hadn't had stable parents growing up. Well, okay, that's not strictly true – Grandma and Grandpa were terrific parent substitutes but this connection was different to how I'd ever felt around *them*. It was hard to comprehend and even harder to keep a firm lid on around others but it was there – an unseen shadow tracing my every move, thought and action.

Ten or maybe fifteen minutes passed with only the mildly static music from the small radio on the windowsill filling the otherwise quiet room until I finally worked up the courage to ask Angie more about herself. I mean, if I was going to try changing things I needed as much background information as possible to go on, right? Besides – it served another more personal purpose too – by finding out more about Angie I'd be discovering a lost part of my heritage – of my roots. I'd spent so long feeling disconnected from any sense of family other than Grandma and Grandpa (and occasionally Dad I suppose), that it felt like the only way to fill a void in my identity.

"What were *you* like when you were a teenager?" I asked eventually.

Angie turned her head round towards me and grinned at the question as if recalling a more care-free time. There was a spark or twinkle in the corner of her eyes that hadn't been there before and after a few seconds of pondering Angie stopped scrubbing the cooker and began inviting me into her past.

"Me? I suppose I was just like any other girl – I loved to dance, I loved music – *Blondie* was my favourite. I remember wanting to be just like Debbie Harry – I'd practice the dance moves to every song I'd see her sing on TV. My favourite song by them has always been *'Dreaming'* – I used to listen to that for hours – in fact, I think I've still got a copy knocking about on cassette." She confessed, looking past me with a gaze that reached back into her past.

"How about when you met James?"

Again her eyes glazed over with some hidden joy of stirred memories.

"Oh, when I met James I knew I was in love. He used to wear this studded punk leather jacket over a white tee and faded blue jeans. Whenever he'd get the chance, he'd put the jukebox on and we'd dance around the tables and barstools – those moments felt like forever. You know, I can remember the first time I took James home to meet my parents – he was so nervous. Dad didn't take to him at first but when he saw that James wasn't a 'phase' I was going through he softened up a little."

"Was it just you and your parents then?"

"Oh no, I've got a sister – Karen. It sure as hell takes a bright star to eclipse her, I can tell you; always having to go one better than everyone else."

And just like that – I had an aunt. One I'd never even known about nor would have known about if it hadn't been for me having this conversation with Angie. And though I got the distinct impression of sibling rivalry between the two of them, it was great to know that I had more family out there. Perhaps I could even get to meet them if I could sort out whatever's supposed to go wrong.

"Have you always wanted to get into business management? I remember you mentioning it at Linda's."

"Not always. I was adrift for a long time but then...and don't you *dare* repeat this...when Margaret Thatcher won the '79 election it opened my eyes and showed me that women *could* achieve anything they wanted to if they worked hard enough at it. From then on I *knew* I wanted to climb the corporate ladder and achieve the best of my potential. Turns out I was in the right place at the right time too – the Eighties saw a surge in women establishing a presence in management-level business and that's when I got my first big break."

"So where do you work?" I asked.

"I landed a job at a private investment company in London. They're on the Times 100 – Carter Reeves and Partners. At the moment I'm a PA, that's 'Personal Assistant' by the way, for the Assistant Director of HR – Simon. But that's not the best thing...he's agreed a training plan for me where the company will sponsor me to go to university and earn a degree in business management or any specialism I choose. Simon reckons I could even be on the board of directors one day."

As I listened to her I realised just how enraptured she was in her goal of making it big in business and building a career for herself. She sounded so positive, so full of determination, hope and ambition that at that moment she could have accomplished anything. Angie sure enough had hopes and dreams and by sharing them with me she came to life in a whole new way – this wasn't just Angie: my mother or partner of James, *this* was an Angie fuelled by a revitalised sense of purpose and vigour. For years I had a picture of her in my mind and right now, listening to her as she spoke about her goals and aspirations, that picture came to life – in vivid colour and magnificent splendour.

"Yeah – I wanna make this work," she said determinedly, "I'm going to make something of myself."

I took the opportunity to learn as much as I could about Mum and her life – wilfully absorbing every miniscule detail like a sponge. I wish I could have told her who I was but just being here and talking to her was enough to make me feel closer to her. She was Angie, and she was my Mum.

We carried on cleaning while we talked until at last the flat was clean from top to bottom and I'd learnt everything Angie had cared to share about herself. And in a light-hearted moment, she dug out the cassette tape she'd told me about earlier and put it on before encouraging me to dance along with her as she showed off the dance moves she'd memorised years earlier. It was surreal but such a rush – here I was dancing along to *Blondie* with the mother I was just getting to know. And even though I must have looked a total prat dancing out of step and trying unsuccessfully to follow Angie's lead, I didn't care. This moment was beyond compare and one I'd treasure always.

*   *   *

I left the flat around 2 in the afternoon – leaving Angie still dancing away to songs from her youth, and made my way to Artie's Cafe to meet Charlotte and Josh. When I arrived Grace was cheerfully tending the counter while looking over at the sound of the door chime I'd set off.

"How have you been?" she asked while fixing me a drink.

I didn't really understand why Grace asked me questions like that – after all, as an Angel of Destiny you'd pretty much know the answers already but I guess it was her attempt at getting me to think about things and so I mustered a reply. There was so much I wanted to tell her that I stopped silent for a moment while processing which bit to say first.

"I saw them again, Grace, my parents – I'm learning so much about them but I'm still no closer to working out what went wrong in the first place or how to change things."

"Give it time, honey. After all, Rome wasn't built in a day." she offered soothingly as she passed my drink across the counter to me.

"No, they did night shifts as well." I shot back with a smile.

Grace chuckled before turning her attention to something behind her as I took hold of the cold smooth glass and turned to observe the rest of the cafe. To my surprise I saw Charlotte slumped glumly in a booth on the far side of the cafe – absently nursing a drink while looking like she had the weight of the world upon her shoulders. I recalled the cryptic conversation we'd had yesterday when I'd found her in a similar frame of mind; there was obviously something important to her going on and I wanted to help if I could.

"Hey," I smiled as I slid into the opposite side of the booth.

"Oh, hey Luke." came the somewhat distant reply.

"Look...it's clear something's getting to you and I wanna help if I can but I don't know how."

"Neither do I." She answered with a strong hint of sadness in her eyes.

"Well, do you wanna talk about it?"

"Oh Luke — I don't know how I can do this. I...I thought I could, that it'd be so easy but it's so hard...and every second I waste brings it closer. I just don't know what to do."

"About what?" I probed softly.

Charlotte turned her head away slightly as small crystal-clear tears began streaming down her cheeks — forcing her to wipe them dry with the sleeve of her denim jacket; and succumbing to a surge of sympathy I shuffled round next to her and stretched one arm around her slender shoulders, holding her close to show that she wasn't alone.

"Hey...whatever it is you don't have to face it alone. *I'm* here for you and so is Josh." I offered supportively.

She sighed bemused while still fighting the tears — as if I had inadvertently said something darkly humorous. After a few seconds she must have noticed my confused expression as she squeezed my hand tenderly before lightly pulling away and composing herself.

"Where were you before, Luke?" she mused aloud, "Why don't I know you?"

I got an uncomfortable notion of what she was driving at and offered a bemused smile in a bid to evade having to explain away my being here in 1990 although it did puzzle me why Charlotte didn't seem to have that same foggy pseudo-recollection of me that everyone else here had — just like Grace had mentioned. Nevertheless I tried to steer the conversation back to what was troubling Charlotte — determined to be of some help, however limited or miniscule.

"What matters is that I'm here now," I affirmed, "Now who or what is getting to you?"

Charlotte once again cast her gaze away from me – this time focusing on her drink as she absently ran one finger around its rim.

"You wouldn't believe me."

"How do you know that?!" I asked, confused.

"Because if I was where you are right now, *I* wouldn't believe me."

"Try me."

I was determined to get Charlotte to open up – bottling things up inside wasn't doing her any favours and she obviously needed someone right about now so I wasn't about to let her cryptic evasions derail my efforts to help her. The next minute or so was filled with Charlotte looking at me nervously – as if weighing up the dangers of offering me an insight into her problems before she finally took a deep, cleansing breath and began opening up to me.

"What I'm about to say might sound strange but I swear it's the truth, okay? Something's going to happen to Josh and I *need* to stop it." She offered in a tone so serious it commanded every ounce of my attention.

"What do you mean? I don't understand?"

"He's *going* to die, okay, and I *can't* let that happen."

Cold chills trickled down my spine as what she said began to sink in. Of all the things I'd been expecting her to say, *that* hadn't even been an outsider. She was so serious, so resolute as if, for her, it was an established fact. None of this made any sense.

"How do you know this? Was it a dream...or..."

"No, okay, it's *not* a dream, it's a *fact* – Josh dies sometime within the next few weeks. I know its going to happen because it already *has* happened – at least for me. You see, I've loved Josh for a long time and I can't let him die...not again."

The hairs on the back of my neck all stood to attention and held themselves erect as if in stasis as Charlotte's revelation hit my like an oncoming freight-train. And then an explanation came to me and I thought aloud...

"Bloody hell -you're from the future, aren't you?!" I grinned.

It was amazing – I wasn't the only one here that wasn't from this time and I suddenly realised what Grace had meant when she'd said that my destiny intersects with another. That other was...Charlotte. This was all happening too fast but I had to keep pace, had to make sense of what was going on in order to stand any chance of being successful here in 1990.

Misinterpreting my response as a rejection, Charlotte huffed and got up to leave – noticeably frustrated.

"I knew you wouldn't believe me. Just...forget I said anything, okay?! And if you repeat this to anyone I'll deny it."

Reaching out, I lightly but firmly took a hold of her forearm to stop her storming off. When I next looked into her eyes I saw the sadness, passion and loneliness in her gaze – which drew an alarming parallel with what I saw whenever I looked in a mirror.

"I never said I didn't believe you." I offered softly.

"Oh really?! And just why *would* you believe me, anyway?"

"Because...*I'm* from the future too."

Naively I'd expected her to accept me at my word and calm down, although looking back; I can understand why, under the circumstances, it didn't quite work out as I planned. By now she looked even more incensed and offended – like I'd stoked whatever fire was burning away inside her.

"Don't you dare make fun of me, Luke. You have no idea what I'm going through."

And with that Charlotte tried pulling away from my grasp but, desperate to convince her that I was being honest and sincere, I reaffirmed my grip on her forearm – prompting her, at least in the short-term to stay and listen to what I had to say next. I knew I had to convince her, but how? I had to think of something fast that would prove I wasn't from 1990 and so, working from memory I began recounting historical details post-1990 in rapid-fire succession that would validate my claim.

"1991 – *Nirvana* single-handedly define 'grunge' with *"Smells Like Teen Spirit"* – a few years later front-man Kurt Cobain dies – long before his time. 1993 – the film adaptation of 'Jurassic Park' is released and heralded for its ground-breaking special effects. The most memorable scene is the one with the shaking glass of water. 1997 – Labour wins a landslide victory in the General Election and Princess Diana tragically dies while in Paris during the summer. Additionally, *Radiohead* release the fantastic album *"OK Computer"* which coincidently becomes one of my favourites. 2001 – the worst terrorist attacks in recent history hit the continental United States – provoking what the President later terms as the *'War on Terror'*. Also in that year, US corporate giant *Enron* collapses following a monumental and unprecedented accounting scandal. 2008 – so-called 'toxic debt' brings the western economy to the brink of collapse – sparking the worst recession since the Great Depression of the 1930s. 2009 – Chicago senator Barack Obama makes history after being sworn-in as the first black President of the United States. 2010 – after an indecisive General Election here in Britain, two of the major parties band together to form a coalition government – the first the country has seen in decades."

Charlotte looked at me with her eyes and mouth wide open in amazement and disbelief before cracking a wry smile to show me that I'd convinced her.

"Is that as far as you go?"

"Well...yeah. Why? When do *you* come from?"

"A fair way after that." She answered cryptically.

And with that Charlotte sat back down and looked at me silently – observing me in a different way than she had done before. It was amazing and surreal – there were two of us: two travellers – both here at the same point in time but apparently from different points in the future. It was the stuff of dreams but here – *now* – it was real.

From then on we became amazed with the other's story and talked at length about all the trivial things that seem weird between 1990 and where we'd each come from – buildings and shops that had either gone completely or regenerated beyond recognition; streets that either weren't built yet or still being developed – along with the housing complexes that were destined to adorn them. It was so funny talking to someone who actually knew Sutton as I remembered it from 2010 – although the 1990 era Sutton did have a certain charm that had been diminished with the town's move into the 21st century, but still.

"So why are *you* here? After all, you weren't originally in 1990, were you?" Charlotte asked eventually.

"Well, yes and no…I *was* but not like this. I was born in '89 and I'm here because something around this time happens that ends up separating me from my parents."

She looked at me sympathetically and lightly squeezed one hand supportively.

"So have you seen them? Your parents I mean?"

"Yeah," I replied enthusiastically, "And they're so cool. Get this – I even got to babysit my younger self."

"No way – that's so mad."

"Tell me about it! But the upside was I got to go to my parent's place. I'm trying to learn all I can about them but I'm still no closer to working out what went wrong or how to stop it."

"I know that feeling. I really *was…am* 15 in 1990," Charlotte said, getting noticeably confused with her tenses given our unique situation, "But I don't know what happened to Josh – like, what caused his death, no one does. At least, no details were ever released. And it's been so long. So I'm feeling pretty lost too."

"That's awful," I said, returning the sympathetic hand-squeezing gesture while realising that *that* was why Josh wasn't in the future and why I didn't know him before coming here, "How much time have you got?"

"I…I'm not sure. But it's soon. I know he doesn't live to see the summer. Over the years I guess I've buried most of what happened but being back here…seeing Josh again…it's shaking some of those memories loose."

With that, Charlotte turned her head away for a moment – forcibly composing herself amidst the threat of another volley of tears and she swallowed a growing lump in her throat before turning back to face me again.

"I've always regretted not telling Josh how much I love him. I've never loved anyone else the way I loved him." She added soulfully.

"There's still time. He's still alive – *here...now*. And we'll make sure he stays that way – *together*, okay?"

A glimmer of hope sparkled in her eyes as her faith began to regroup until at last a faint but determined smile blossomed once again on her youthful face.

"You mean it?"

"Yeah, I do. Josh is family and you're like *the* only person in this time that understands me fully – well, except Grace but she has an advantage what with being an Angel of Destiny and all."

And within a second of mentioning Grace, our resident Angel of Destiny appeared next to us – standing at the end of the table with a serious expression on her face. She didn't look cross – more like concerned as she repositioned her glasses before taking a breath and exclaiming aloud.

"I knew this would happen. I told them. I told them not to send me two charges so closely linked – it's too risky."

"What do you mean?" asked Charlotte.

"Hey, why didn't you tell me that Charlotte was another traveller like me?"

Looking as if she had the weight of the world upon her shoulders, Grace sighed before continuing, "I mean it's risky having two people trying to change connected timelines at the same time. Normally in the grand scheme of things what each of you are aiming to achieve wouldn't be a problem but in this case there are certain...complications."

"What type of complications?" I asked.

"The fact that your destinies here are interlinked – not altogether one and same you understand but close enough for it to become problematic. You see, the changes you each aim to make will largely affect the same people who, in each circumstance would become dependent upon another. For example in the current timeline when Josh dies it forces Linda to withdraw completely to the point where she's not there for Luke's Dad when the inevitable happens between him and Angie..."

"It's not inevitable, Grace. I'm going to change that." I added indignantly.

Grace looked at me as if she knew things about the situation that I did not. It wasn't a pitiful look but one of regret that I didn't yet know what she did and she shot a faint smile in my direction as if not wanting to dash my hopes.

"Perhaps," she offered, "But nevertheless – the lives affected by the changes you'll make will overlap and have repercussions. Imagine time like a boulder teetering on the edge of a cliff with each of you pushing the boulder in different directions – trying to stop it from falling over the edge. Now, because you're each pushing in a different direction you inadvertently run the risk of the boulder tipping over the edge anyway despite your best efforts. Life is like...an equation – it *needs* to balance and if you change too much you risk unbalancing it and *that* is very dangerous."

"Dangerous how?"

"Well, sooner or later that boulder's gonna fall *somewhere* and *that* will have ripple effects also and so on. That's why people don't normally get the chance you two have been given because it can be too risky."

"So what are you saying? Are you saying we're *not* allowed to change things, now?" asked Charlotte.

"What I'm saying is that the pair of you need to be extremely careful with *what* you change."

"But we *can* still change things though, right?"

"Yes *but*…not everything *can* be changed. Certain events are destined to happen for other reasons – a higher purpose and reasons of a similar ilk. But the most important changes – major things with long-reaching implications are only possible through sacrifice – remember; the equation *always* needs to balance. It's a fundamental rule."

It was a lot to take in and I'd be lying if I said I completely understood all that Grace had explained. It was one of those things that sort-of makes sense but the deeper you go the more mind-blowing and complicated it gets and right now I was determined to keep things simple: keep my parents together; save Josh and go home. It sounded so simple when I thought of it that way. Besides, what could possibly go wrong?

Grace declined to offer any specifics on what each of us should do or indeed expand upon what could and could not be changed here in 1990 – leaving it up to our individual speculation, which depending on your perspective could be better or worse than just being told outright.

When Grace eventually returned to her normal spot behind the counter, Charlotte and I continued comparing notes on how strange we'd been finding being in 1990 – it was different for her though, she'd been here before, so I guess for her it was more a sense of semi-humorous nostalgia mixed with her comparably more serious purpose for being here; whereas it was different for me – I hadn't been here first-time round, not like this at least, so there was a greater sense of curious detachment in dealing with this familiar and yet distant environment.

"D'you know – *I'm* almost old enough to be your mum," joked Charlotte.

Laughing lightly I fell back against the plush leather back of the booth, letting my head fall into my hands in mock horror. She was right – she was bordering on 16 so it was almost a possibility. Man, this time-travel stuff was just outright weird, plain and simple!

"Oh that's just wrong!"

"Seriously though, what was it like meeting your Mum for the first time?" she asked, wide-eyed in curiosity.

"Honestly?" I mused, "It was like that feeling you get on Christmas morning but multiplied by every year I haven't seen her."

"Aww..."

That moment of shared empathy and contemplation must have lasted longer than either of us perceived it and it was true to say that we each became engrossed with happier thoughts and prospects whilst staring towards one another; each linked by a common twist of fate – of our endeavours of circumstance and aspirations until a familiar voice brought us back to the reality of Artie's Cafe...

"Hey, what's going on?"

It was Josh – standing where Grace had been earlier, dressed in a matching hat and scarf bearing the colours of local football team Sutton United. Of course – Saturday – match day. From the slightly awkward expression on Josh's face I guess he must have noticed Charlotte's plutonic grasp of my hand and thought that there was more to it as Charlotte quickly withdrew it and looked towards him with a heart-warming smile.

"Nothing, we were just...talking. So – you all set for the match then?" Charlotte replied warmly.

"Yeah, we'll get going in a minute, I'll have a drink first though."

After what I now knew it was hard to look at Josh – at that face – in those eyes and imagine them lifeless. Although, without intervention, that is precisely what would happen. He couldn't die. He just couldn't. He was young and full of dreams. He deserved a full life and I was determined to help Charlotte ensure he got it.

"What's up with *you*, Luke? You look like you've seen a ghost."

Chapter Six

Josh led the way from the High Street over to West Sutton where the team home-ground was. I don't think I'd ever seen Josh as enthused as he was now – suited up in his team-branded woolly hat and scarf. He looked so full of life and so happy that again it wasn't possible to visualise a time when he would be anything other than that.

"Ah, I've been waiting for this *all* week. Honestly, sometimes I thought Saturday would *never* come." Josh said, wracked with anticipation as we walked through the back streets.

"Aww bless, look...he's all excited." I teased playfully.

Charlotte grinned, preferring to remain a silent observer, at least for the moment.

"Sod off." Josh shot back at me with a smile.

 "Well I for one think it's sweet. Some men have a dog or a car to get engrossed in but Josh has a football team." added Charlotte, coming to her beau's aid.

"Thanks," replied Josh, feigning apprehension, "...I think!"

We all laughed – bound by a common sense of kinship and humour. I know in reality I was a stranger to them but in the short time that I had come to know Josh and Charlotte I felt closer to them than anyone I had ever befriended. It was through them that the cold defensiveness I'd built up around myself began to thaw. For so long I'd held on to the notion of not letting anyone (other than Grandma and Grandpa) close to me for fear of eventually being cast adrift in the same way that Dad had cast me adrift. But here, with them, that cold detachment was thawing – allowing me to reach out and connect with people in a way I'd never felt brave enough to before.

By the time we arrived it was near kick-off as Josh suddenly became largely unrecognisable amidst the fluidic carpet of fans moving in large clusters, all clad in similar team-branded hats and scarves. There were even running chants of "We love you Sutton, we do…" floating about like a clarion call summoning the supporters to gather a sporting equivalent of Mass. And the stadium, whilst not being as grandiose or lavish as some of its contemporaries, held a unique local team feeling – seemingly a world away from the big money and transfer politics that were rife in other spheres of Britain's national game. But most of all, this place felt like somewhere people could gather to play or support the game purely for the enjoyment of it. It was an unspoilt example of what would become marginalised as the world stumbled into the twenty-first century.

As Josh was the only one who knew his way around the grounds, he again led the way until Charlotte stopped at the sight of someone she knew across the crowd.

"You two go ahead – I'm gonna catch up with Rachel." She announced.

"Aren't we kinda in the middle of something?" I asked, subtlety glancing in Josh's direction.

"I *really* need to talk with her. You two go ahead. I'll see you in a bit."

From Charlotte's tone it was clear that something more was going on with this friend of hers – somehow Charlotte felt compelled to interact at a point where I'm guessing she didn't originally. If that was the case and Charlotte was attempting to alter something, even something seemingly minor or done with the best of intentions then she needed to be careful. Grace had been very explicit about us altering the timeline. Not everything *could* be changed here – some things were just destined to be.

At that point I didn't quite know what to do. Charlotte was the only one out of the two of us that had first-hand knowledge of this time and the events that happened here and by her sudden opting to indulge some spur of the moment deviation I immediately felt WAY out of my depth. In that moment the pressure and responsibility of looking after Josh seemed like too big a burden to bare alone and paradoxically I realised how suffocating it must be for Charlotte. But those doubts wouldn't leave me alone – what if whatever happened to him happened here, now? Or if he came into contact with someone or thing that was somehow pivotal to what transpires? What if I wasn't able to save him alone? Damn, this was hard work.

Utterly oblivious to the serious subtext to what was going on, Josh merely shrugged casually before lightly slapping me on one arm.

"Okay. Looks like it's just you and me then, Luke."

As Josh began walking away I stayed for a moment – looking at Charlotte and saying with my gaze all the things that my lips couldn't or wouldn't dare say aloud.

"Sorry" she mouthed silently.

I half smiled and sighed in response. It was the only reply I could muster before she turned to fight her way through the crowd towards her friend. Suddenly I began getting a churning sensation in my stomach which was amplified by the war-drum beat of the supporters' chants and claps. As the anxiety within me grew, the situation began feeling like a runaway train rolling relentlessly down the line towards the inevitable happenstance that would force it from the tracks.

When the match started the electric feeling amongst the fans was amplified – with each side gathered like tribal groups, poised to watch with fevered anticipation as their chosen warriors competed for superiority. Each kick, pass and tackle was savoured and celebrated (depending which side you were on) and it was hard not to get into the spirit of it. In fact, every so often Josh would look round and prompt me to get involved.

"Josh, tell Charlotte how you feel about her."

Part of me felt like I was interfering in something that wasn't my business but I'd seen how their denial of their feeling towards each other was tearing them apart. They danced around each other like some ballroom foxtrot every time they spoke – with the connotations of truth and meaning constantly living beneath the surface – in the subtext of their conversations. In Charlotte's case I knew that she had never felt for anyone the way she does for Josh – hell, she'd come goodness-knows how many years back in time just to save him from a premature death – if *that* doesn't say you love someone then I'm not sure what does.

"What?!" he replied, "No..."

"Why not?"

"Because...because what if it changes things or ruins what we have right now?"

"What if it doesn't?" I countered.

"Life's no fairytale, Luke. Ha! In fact, the last thing I'd want is for me and Charlotte to turn out like Uncle James and Angie."

The sudden reference to my parents threw me for a second. Why would Josh say something like that? What did he know about my parents that I didn't? Truthfully, there was a part of me that didn't want to know what was wrong between them – a part that wanted to cling to the romanticised image of them I'd come to adopt since being here but the future – *my* future – told me that there was some substance or at least relevance to Josh saying what he did and so I had to know more.

"What do you mean?"

"She doesn't love him – at least not anymore."

"What?! That's rubbish!" I replied indignantly, fighting to be heard above the now chanting crowd.

"It's true," Josh answered when the chants subsided, "the amount of times he's come round to ours in tears, sitting up with Mum until all hours. But even with all the crap Angie gives him he still loves her. Poor sod."

"You're lying!" I exclaimed, refusing to let my view of my parent's relationship be tainted.

"Luke, why would I lie? I love Uncle James – he's cool. I just think love can end up screwing some people up and I don't want that to happen to me and Charlotte – I'd rather have the dream."

I couldn't quite take what Josh said in; at least not well, anyway. The mere notion of my parents being in a loveless or partially-loveless relationship just wasn't possible. They'd loved each other enough to have me hadn't they so what had changed? Why would it? It didn't make sense.

"Alright – forget James, forget Angie. Josh – you love Charlotte. You know you do, so stop beating about the bush and tell her already or one day it might be too late."

And then finally it appeared as if Josh was warming to the idea as his face flashed a sense of deep contemplation while he continued watching the game. Minutes passed before he spoke again but when he did I could tell he was finally lowering whatever barrier it was that had been preventing him from confessing how he felt sooner.

"I trust you, yeah. Honestly now, do you *really* think it's a good idea?"

"Yes – of course. Josh, there are people the world over who spend their entire lives regretting not saying it. Don't let yourself become one of them."

"GOAL!" Josh exclaimed suddenly – looking at the pitch before focusing back on our conversation, "I guess you're right. I'd be dead without her."

And now it was *my* turn to exclaim!

"Whoa! Whoa! Nobody is gonna die, okay? Nobody!"

It was only afterwards that I realised how extreme my reaction had been. Ever since Charlotte decided to take her little detour earlier on I'd been so fixated on making sure Josh stayed alive that his mention of his own death, albeit in a different context, had set all manner of alarm bells ringing in my head. But obviously to Josh, my outburst seemed a million miles removed from ordinary.

"*What* the hell?!" he chuckled as he looked at me with eyes as wide open as two full moons.

"Sorry, I'm...a bit touchy about death." I lied plausibly with a brief smile, "It...creeps me out."

The match lasted another forty minutes or so after that and when the match had finished, we casually drifted back to *Artie's* after having to track Charlotte down in the football club's social lounge – the "*Boom Boom Club*". From the look on her face she had a profound impact upon events that were about to unfold around her friend. I couldn't blame her really – if that had been me I'd of probably done the same thing, even despite Grace's warning about disrupting life's tapestry too much.

Josh had confided in me late on during the match that he was going to tell Charlotte how he felt about her but was unsure about how. I'd given him the suggestion of choosing a location that was significant to both of them; setting the mood with music and then letting his heart do the talking. In truth it was probably mirrored some scene I'd seen or read about but it seemed to serve a valid purpose in this context. Obviously Josh was nervous about whether or not his feelings would be reciprocated but, being party to privileged knowledge, I did my best to encourage him and the walk to *Artie's* gave him the necessary time and space to gather his thoughts and confidence for what was to come. He wouldn't regret it – Charlotte loved Josh just as much as he loved her – they were right for each other – like they were 'meant to be'.

Still, Josh's remarks about my parents clung to me with tar-like longevity. He hadn't been lying – I knew him well enough by now to know when he was lying or joking and when he wasn't. Besides, he had no stake in my parent's relationship so that ruled out intentional malice; so then why had he said what he did? From the little I knew of Angie I was adamant that somehow Josh must be mistaken. Mum…*and* Dad were both great people – so much so that it was inconceivable that anything could go wrong, even though I knew it had…and *would* again unless I could alter things.

The bell above the door chimed as Josh, Charlotte and I entered *Artie's* in the small, picturesque shopping arcade off the High Street; and upon entering the three of us began to disperse in different directions: Charlotte gravitated (as though on autopilot) towards a booth seat at the back of the café; Josh, following similar-ish trajectory veered towards the 1950's-esque jukebox and began flipping through the song lists while I approached the main counter and walked into the heart-warming embrace of Grace's infectious smile.

"Hey"

"Hey," I replied, "Have you got a moment?"

"Sure, what's on your mind?"

In the near background the opening melody of Thompson Twins hit "Hold Me Now" roared into life from the vintage jukebox. From the extensive introduction it sounded like the extended 12" mix, which I knew because Dad had this on record and had played it occasionally back when he'd briefly lived with me, Grandma and Grandpa years ago. I looked over my shoulder briefly to see the magic moment unfold before focusing back on Grace.

"Josh, what's going on? I don't understand..." came Charlotte's voice.

"Charlotte, there's something I've got to tell you..." he answered, slipping into the space next to her on the squashy leather booth seat.

Turning back, I noticed Grace also looking discreetly over at the two lovers as she continued tending the main counter, with a distinct look of satisfaction – as if she too had also been waiting for that moment to happen.

"Grace, I'm not sure I'm able to change things. It seems like I've been here forever and things are *still* happening as they did originally."

"Not everything," she replied with a discreet nod in Josh and Charlotte's direction.

"You know what I mean – with my parents. It seems like I'm having zero effect at the moment and then earlier Josh said that Mum doesn't love Dad anymore – is that true?"

Grace's smile faded momentarily as she uncharacteristically became short of words whilst considering her response.

"It's complicated. People tend to see things in a linear fashion but life isn't a two-dimensional perspective – there are things going on all around us, some of which we don't even see or pick up on. With your parents, they're both victims of circumstance. Life brought them together but there are forces at work that are now driving them apart." She offered eventually.

"But I *can* change that right? I mean, that's why I'm here..."

"It's not that simple, Luke. I'm sorry."

"So…*what*? I *can't* change things?" I uttered, confused.

"I didn't say that."

"But if I can't keep them together then what's the point of all this?"

Grace shot me a sympathetic glance in much the same way a parent would when trying to reassure a child of something. In many ways I guess I was still a child – at least inside. There had always been a part of me that seemed to be frozen in childhood – waiting for my parents to make everything normal again – to make *me* normal again, but at the age of twenty-one I was still waiting and still had that part of my psyche, my being frozen at an earlier stage of development.

"Oh Luke, sweetheart, you *can* still change some things for the better, I've never denied that – but, that's not necessarily the same as *your* ideal of what would be better. Remember – life's not about the destination it's about the journey."

Somehow, even though not giving any specifics, her words seemed to quell the raging torrent of anxiety inside me and I began drawing comfort from her reassurance that things could be turned around – even if that turnaround didn't match what I had envisioned.

"Why can't you tell me what happens, Grace?" I asked longingly.

"Hey, I don't make the rules I just 9-to-5 them. There are things that you need to discover yourself. I may not be able to tell you everything but I *am* here for you. It's what destiny's about – I can guide you but I can't directly intervene without an air-tight reason – you have to be solely responsible for your own actions, that's why God gave people free-will."

"What happened to 'ask and ye shall receive'?!" I replied with a cheeky smirk.

"You got the chance to come back and make a difference, didn't you?" Grace smiled, "Besides, if you're throwing Biblical justification into this then wasn't it Jesus who told a previously crippled man he healed to 'get up and walk'? Some things we just have to do ourselves."

I suppose to an outsider it would have appeared as if we were seriously quarrelling but it was all light-hearted, albeit with a serious subtext. Besides, Grace was an angel – literally – so compassion and understanding were in her job description.

"Alright, you win," I sighed playfully, "I guess there *are* things I need to work out by myself."

And with that Grace took a hold of my right hand as she gazed at me with pure empathy and support in her eyes.

"Luke," she said, "you can do this. It'll be hard dealing with some of the things you'll come up against but you *can* do it and it'll be worth it. You deserve to be happy so don't let doubt cloud that. You're here to make a difference and that's exactly what you're going to do."

"Thanks Grace." I replied before turning round to see Josh and Charlotte still snuggled up together in a loving embrace, "I'd best be off – when...or *if* they come up for air would you tell them I've gone home and that I'll see them later."

"Sure."

"Thanks Grace – for everything."

"You're welcome."

And so I left Artie's – allowing Josh and Charlotte to share their intimate moment without me there being the proverbial third wheel. As I drifted through the top end of Sutton High Street I thought about how the future knowledge that Charlotte had must be a burden as much as a blessing – to know all that she did and still keep smiling – to keep silent in certain circumstances – and *that* was what made her truly a woman of great strength, resolve and character. As I continued pondering things the gravity of Charlotte's predicament unknowingly lent weight to my own. Suddenly the deceptively simple remit of changing the past seemed a lot more complicated. It wasn't as simple as making a few surgical strikes in a sequence of events, it was altogether more complex with the added consideration of cause and effect, ripple effects and how changing one thing no matter how minor could potentially have far-reaching repercussions; having to ensure that each change would still co-exist harmoniously with the larger chain of causality and circumstance.

In hindsight I don't think anything could have prepared me for what happened next. It was a chance encounter of circumstance and innocence in which innocence was stolen by a savage shot of realism as Grace's earlier advice echoed poignantly through my head. What I saw changed everything and seemed to suck all the colour out of that moment – leaving everything grey and devoid of cheer. Inside, I felt my stomach twist and churn in painful knots as I watched a stranger shatter my perception of all I thought I'd come to know about my parents by intimately taking hold of someone I *thought* I'd come to know.

Frozen in rage and terror I watched helplessly as the stranger's advance was reciprocated and the two shared a private yet equally public moment of romantic affection. Remaining unseen I saw the familiar face in a completely different way. One again she was a stranger to me. She was Angie.

Chapter Seven

That image…that moment stayed with me for hours afterwards – even once I'd reached the relative safety of my room at Linda's house. That fateful encounter replayed over and over before my eyes as I sat aghast on the bed – realising at last the true depth of what had been…*is*…going on. From how Angie and that guy had interacted with each other it was clear that they weren't relatives or even close friends – they were something more – something romantic and that thought turned my entire world upside down. I felt so confused right now that virtually nothing felt certain anymore as my head became flooded under a torrent of questions I couldn't answer: why had she done that? Was that what drove her and Dad apart? And if so then why had Dad also kept largely out my life as well? So many questions without answers – what was I going to do? What could I do? I didn't know.

Angie had been a figure of hope for me for so long that to recognise her now as some fallen idol was heartbreaking. She had been the one I'd pinned my hopes on to make everything right – to bring everything together and now I'd found that she was the very reason everything fell apart. What or who the hell should I believe in now? If Angie couldn't make it right then who could? Why did she have to do this? It didn't make sense and more than that – it wasn't fair. In the past week or so I'd found my mother at long last – only to lose her again to circumstances arising from her own choices. She truly was like a stranger to me again – someone I couldn't relate to anymore. The divide between us was just too great now. But still, the thought that for one precious moment – no matter how fleeting – that

I'd found her provided a strong counter-defence to the anger boiling inside me. Angie had been a star to me for so long, and stars never shone as bright once they fell.

A knock at the bedroom door brought me out of the maelstrom of my thoughts and I saw Auntie Linda poking her head around the door to tell me that dinner was ready. I guess I must have had a face like thunder as she quickly replaced her trademark smile with a less jovial expression and stepped further into the room.

"Luke, sweetheart, whatever's the matter?" she asked sitting down beside me.

"It's my parents…I don't know what's going on except that my Mum's done this thing that will seriously screw up her and Dad. I know they're going to break-up soon and I just don't know what I can do to stop it. It just sucks."

I knew Linda wouldn't know who exactly I was talking about and if I'm honest I don't really know why I was telling her but it helped getting the problem out in the open. It helped that there was someone there to talk about it to.

"Aww, come here," Linda said, reaching over to embrace me, "Sometimes we just have to ride these things out. I know it's tough but things will get better in time."

"There must be something I can do or say. I don't want them to split up."

"Of course you don't sweetheart but the only ones who can truly stop your parents separating *are* your parents."

"So where does that leave me?"

"Loved," she answered, running her hand lightly through my hair, "By *all* of your family. No matter what happens between your Mum and Dad you'll always have family to rely on and who'll love you."

There was an unmistakable warmth to Linda's words – a warmth that held you snugly in it's intangible embrace whilst gently soothing even the darkest of your fears; and in a way I guess she was right – even in the future I'd come from I still have Grandma and Grandpa...and even Dad in this own weird little "part-time" way. But that aside, I knew that I had been brought back to 1990 for a reason – to make some quantifiable, lasting difference; from all that Grace had shared and all that I had learnt while being here it was evident that there *was* something I *could* do – I just hadn't worked out what...*yet*.

*   *   *

Next morning I was woken up a little after eight by an over-excited Josh who stood bathed in light from the landing as he spoke to me from just inside the doorway.

"Hey...get up. Luke...wake up, c'mon."

I grunted in disapproval in the vain hope I could fall back off to sleep again after seeing the time on the digital alarm clock on the bedside table – *08:06* – on a *Sunday*! I turned away from the intrusive beam of light – resolute in the belief that waking up early on a Sunday was simply *not* happening – at least not for me anyway.

But clearly Josh had other ideas as I suddenly felt something firm and soft hit the back of my head and turning over again found it to be a pillow I'd apparently thrown off the bed in my sleep.

"Oh, Josh…what the hell?!" I groaned groggily.

"Get up – we're going to the zoo!" he exclaimed.

"What?!"

"Which part didn't you get?!" Josh answered sarcastically, "C'mon…"

Begrudgingly, I shuffled into a sitting position and rubbed my eyes as they adjusted to the change in light.

"Alright…I'm up."

"Good. Hurry up and get ready. Breakfast'll be ready in ten minutes."

Josh sounded like a kid at Christmas – practically bursting with excitement and playful impatience. Reaching round, I grabbed the pillow he'd thrown at me and launched it back at him playfully.

"Get outta' here!"

I did my level best to concentrate on my appearance but somehow I still seemed to look like I'd just been raised from the dead and went downstairs to breakfast anyway. Uncle Henry was engrossed in his large broadsheet Sunday newspaper while Josh and Auntie Linda were busy tucking into a full-English breakfast as I slipped into the vacant place that had been set for me.

"It's risen! Call the papers!" laughed Josh before negotiating his knife through a sausage.

"Josh – really!" said Auntie Linda, "Good morning Luke. Sleep well?"

"All except for the bit where I was woken up!" I answered sleepily.

"Aww, well it'll be worth it. We're going to the zoo today – a nice family day out. James and baby Luke are coming as well."

"What about Angie?" I asked, feeling my heart questioning whether I'd prefer her there or not.

"Pft! What about her?" came Josh, making his feelings towards Angie evident in his tone.

"Joshua...what have I told you?! Henry, say something..."

Uncle Henry raised his head above the pages of his broadsheet newspaper and looked towards Josh with his glasses resting on the edge of his nose.

"Josh – shut up!" he said, sounding as if he were obliged to offer some comment.

As Josh returned to eating his breakfast, Auntie Linda looked over at me and adopted one of her more diplomatic tones – the type that evidently masked some hidden layer of thought or feeling.

"I...don't think Angie will be joining us today, so it'll just be the six of us including James and the little one. Now, eat up – I said we'd pick up James and Luke around nine."

And so sure enough we left a few minutes after nine to pick up James and the other me (yeah, it's *still* weird about what to call him). When we arrived Angie wasn't there, so I helped Dad down the stairs with the baby-stroller, day-bag and (of course) the baby carrier (complete with baby inside). The journey took the best of an hour, perhaps a little over with the traffic along the way, but eventually we arrived at London Zoo all hyped for a great family day out. Auntie Linda had driven there, leaving James and Uncle Henry to discuss every random thing from recent experiences with power tools to the news while Josh entertained baby Luke in-between sporadic conversations with me.

Once we'd arrived at the zoo Josh and I huddled next to the car as James and Uncle Henry wrestled the baby stroller into submission; meanwhile Linda and James light-heartedly argued over who was paying for what.

As it turned out, the zoo proved to be a much-needed distraction from everything else that was going on. It seemed that all bar my worries over Dad, everything from back home in Sutton was left at the gate. My head was so messed up right now that I wasn't sure what to do to be right – part of me wanted to guard Dad against the pain of what Angie was doing and just tell him outright and yet something continually stopped me. Seeing him here, now happy – I didn't want to do anything to alter that and yet the paradox was that I had to alter some things in order for this version of him to still be around in 2010. Oh man, this was complicated. All along I'd been hoping I could keep my parents together somehow but in the stark reality of what I had seen first-hand that ideal now lay shattered with my only recourse to put back as many of the pieces as I could – even if that meant letting go of Angie in order to save James – to save Dad.

Then there was the guilt – guilt at being angry at Dad for so long when all along it hadn't been his fault, not really. I'd been so caught up on him being a broken man but now I knew the truth; that it wasn't the *man* that was broken – it was his *heart*. When Angie had inevitably left him he'd lost someone he had truly cared about as well as losing a crucial element of stability in his life. Any stranger in the street could tell from face value just how much James loved Angie – it was written in his smile and in his eyes – that unmistakable twinkle that confessed his every unspoken feeling for her; feelings she didn't deserve – not after what she'd done, anyway. But despite my lack of comprehension I did admire Dad's commitment and loyalty to Angie even if it was misplaced.

We all stopped at the penguin enclosure as baby Luke shrieked with delight and clapped his hands together merrily as the emperor penguins waddled around and dived into the water. Ever keen, James got baby Luke out of the stroller and carried him over the enclosure wall so the little one could get a better view. I stood awe-struck as I observed the two interacting with one another. It was like watching a living photo album play out before your eyes or being inside a home movie; it was magical and I savoured every fleeting second of it unashamedly.

When the others went to visit the reptile house, James, baby Luke and myself opted to wait outside. It was curious as to just how similar Dad and I were as we virtually mirrored each other's actions of repulsion and apprehension when telling the others we'd stay outside. I guess I *was* more like him that I'd realised before and somehow that thought was oddly comforting. It wasn't long before James suggested taking the little one to the petting zoo and, having no-where else to go, I tagged along – pleased for the time I was getting to spend getting to know Dad – even if he *didn't* know who I was here.

And being the ever-engaged father in this timeline, James hovered around baby Luke – helping him pet the assortment of small animals, to which my younger self was delighted – with shrieks and smiles communicating his joy.

As this warm scene continued to dance before my eyes I became overwhelmed by the urge to reach out to Dad – here, now. But how? How could I bridge the gap that (for me) had grown stronger over twenty or so years? Maybe it was seeing James interact with baby Luke that suggested a way in, maybe it was the burning desire I'd harboured for wanting to know my parents better; either way, I plucked up the courage and began making an attempt to reach out – for me, for understanding, for something to take away the pain that dwelt inside day after day.

"What do you reckon he'll be....when he grows up, I mean?" I asked curiously.

"Honestly? I don't mind as long as he's happy and safe. You see, other people look at their children and see a doctor or a teacher or a leader but when I look at Luke I just see my son and no amount of career-related fantasies can supersede that."

"I've never known what my Dad wants of me. He keeps himself withdrawn – a lot of the time it's like he doesn't even recognise I exist." I said, keeping myself composed amidst the duality of the conversation.

James turned his head towards me while still tending to his infant son and frowned sympathetically.

"I'm sure that's not how it is, Luke. Any father would be proud of you, I know I would be."

"You would?"

It was surreal – this was the deepest conversation I had ever had with my Dad and the ironic thing was that I was nothing more than a casual stranger to him here. I'd spent years waiting for Dad to say something like that – to validate my existence and prove that I wasn't some mistake he'd rather forget.

"Sure. You're a smart and caring young man. What parent could ask for more?"

At that point I felt an involuntary urge to make a sniping comment about Angie but I suppressed it and kept myself in this moment.

"I dunno. I seem to screw up so much. I've been so angry at my parents for not getting involved in my life that that anger has come to define me – it gets me into so much crap and I hate that." I confessed.

"Take it from me, Luke, your anger *doesn't* define you – your good nature does. People screw up, even your parents – it's just part of being human. The real trick is to accept those imperfections and carry on being who you truly are. You can't make an omelette without breaking a few eggs. Luke, sometimes family don't work to a blueprint, sometimes they go...awry but that doesn't have to derail everything else."

Everything Dad was saying made sense and, though I hadn't been close to him up until now, I couldn't help but trust him implicitly - it was a natural instinct that screamed out from within – an instinct I hadn't been acquainted with before.

"I just want my parents to take an interest in me. I know my Mum doesn't have any intention of doing that – she never wanted a family but my Dad, he's haunted by something and that keeps him distant – in his own little world."

"Well, don't give up on him."

"I don't intend to."

*   *   *

Once we'd met up with the others a bit later on, we continued walking around the zoo – seeing the big cats, elephants and rhinos before eventually stopping at one of the picnic areas. Uncle Henry bought us all a hotdog while James fed baby Luke on the next table along with a small jar of something orange that looked positively revolting.

"They're really close, aren't they?" I said to Auntie Linda while everyone else was occupied.

"Luke is the best thing that ever happened to James. James dotes on him – he's so proud." Linda replied, "It meant the world to James to have a child of his own. I suppose it was his way of balancing out things from his past. Luke's his little miracle."

"What do you mean?"

Auntie Linda leaned in closer and hushed her tone before continuing, "James was adopted. Mum and Dad adopted him when he was about five or six. He's never spoken about his childhood before being adopted but he's clearly haunted by it."

Aghast, I sat there as Linda's words sunk in. I'd never known that about Dad – he must have felt so alone and suddenly, as if a great fog had lifted, all of his bouts of self-imposed isolation made sense. Grandma Irene and Grandpa John had been loving parents to him and supported him since his adoption but Dad was obviously haunted by the abandonment of his biological family and...

"So then his brother?" I thought aloud.

"...Was adopted separately – a few months before James apparently."

"That's awful."

"Yeah, but it was different times back then sweetheart. Don't let on I told you though, okay?"

"Okay."

After that it was hard not to acknowledge the overwhelming sense of respect and understanding I now had for Dad. He'd gone through all of that and still found it within himself to be a loving and engaging father. I wanted to go over to him right now and apologise for all the times I'd thought he was a bad father or that he didn't care, but instead I let that guilt fuel the drive to make things better – harnessing it so that it became a constructive, almost motivational source of energy with which to elicit change. Regardless of what Angie...Mum...no, Angie was up to I was determined to ensure I kept Dad on track – anything less would be a cruel injustice. Again the now familiar irony hit me again – Mum had been the one I'd always believed could set things right and here, now, where she was still around – *she* was the very reason it could nosedive at a moment's notice. I knew it *would* happen – I was living proof of that. I *had* to make a difference. Somehow, someway I had to do something that could save the situation and I began pondering what Grace had told me the other day about change coming with a price. What was my price for changing things? Would I have to sacrifice knowing Mum in order to save Dad? I hoped not. I hoped that I could still have both of them and that we could be a family but I was beginning to absorb other things Grace had shared with me – that even time-travel or divine intervention can't alter some things. Some things *had* to happen, *had* to play out as they always would have. It felt like having to lose Mum in order to save Dad and that sucked. Secretly I was still hoping that I was wrong about that – wrong that that was just the way things were.

Chapter Eight

The next week was actually fairly sedate compared to my arrival. I was getting closer to James whenever he'd visit Linda's and school was…well, school. I was growing to like being in 1990 and did my level best to fit in despite finding the datedness of certain things vaguely humorous and making the occasional faux-pas when saying something that only someone from my time would understand, but that aside, I was feeling like I belonged, like there was a purpose to why I was here and that felt reassuring.

Josh and Charlotte were now virtually inseparable and every-bit the perfect couple – at school and away from it. In fact, I'd been doing my level best to give the pair of them some space so that they could savour every timeless moment they spent together, which in turn left me plenty of time to reflect on things and gain some perspective on what had to be done elsewhere in 1990. Being here, and by "here" I mean "back in time", was weird and challenging but more than that, it was a life-changing and utterly thrilling experience on so many levels and I was beyond thankful that I had been given this opportunity.

Things between Dad and Angie seemed to be getting rockier, heightening the tension that time was running out. Over the course of the week James must have come to Linda's about four times – mostly late in the evening and so I'd try talking to him wherever possible. James would never tell me much but had grown to trusting me slowly but surely, as if recognising the connection between us. The longer I spent here in 1990 getting to know him and know about him, the more I came to view Dad as a fallen hero – he was a good guy at heart who had fallen victim to the combined existential circumstance of past twinning with present. He was at the precipice staring at the unknown and I really felt sorry for him. In the short time I'd gotten to know him here I'd found a lot of minor and larger points where the two of us were similar and in a way knowing that helped me to connect to him better. And more than anything I was racking my brain to translate those connections to him into some way to save him from becoming the shadow he'd become where I'd come from.

It was late afternoon – maybe about four or half four, anyway – I was in my room listening to a mix-tape Charlotte had made for me to "culturally introduce" me to the era, on a red walkman I'd borrowed from Josh. I didn't know most of the songs but they *were* catchy and every so often I came across a song or group that I either knew, knew *and* loved, or had heard Dad play at some stage. As I became immersed in the music I began wondering about home, 2010. Back there I had a friend, James, who loved nothing better than to immerse himself in good music and revel at being a connoisseur of sound. What that guy didn't know about his specialist genres of music wasn't worth knowing. After that I wondered about Grandma and Grandpa and how they were. Were they still huddled around me in that restaurant or was this all happening in the blink of an eye for them? Had these past few weeks been mere milliseconds for them? I hoped they were okay and I couldn't wait to see them again. I found it was the little things that I'd grown to miss like helping Grandpa make and paint his models; Grandma singing golden oldies while pottering about; and Grandma's shepherd's pie – there was truly no other like Grandma's – nothing else came close. Man, I missed her shepherd's pie.

I was staring at the ceiling still listening to the mix-tape when Auntie Linda knocked on the open door, prompting me to lift the headphones off my ears and respond.

"Hey,"

"Hello sweetheart. There's a phone call for you downstairs."

It took me a moment to register what Linda had said. It was weird – who'd be phoning me? Here? I certainly hadn't given the phone number out, in fact – I don't even think I knew it, not completely. And so it was with peaked curiosity I replied.

"For me? Who is it?"

"It's Josh. He say's its important. But you know Josh, bless him, he thinks its crisis if he misses an episode of *Grange Hill*!"

I grinned. It was true. Josh really *was* like that and I think since I'd been here I'd heard the theme music to that show more times than I had in my entire life before now. So I followed Linda downstairs, bemused at what all the excitement could be about and lifted the receiver to my ear once I'd reached the small ledge at the bottom of the stairs where the phone was housed.

"Hello," I said

"Hey, what took you so long?"

"I was, err…listening to something on the walkman."

"You haven't wasted the batteries, have you? There's a new album I wanna listen to on that."

"No Josh, I haven't wasted the batteries."

"Oh, right, good. Err…has Mum set the video to record 'Grange Hill' for me?"

"You called to ask me *that*?!"

"No, but…has she?"

"Yeah, I guess."

"You guess?!" he exclaimed.

"Josh, what the hell?! What do you want?"

"What, oh right – yeah, sorry…Charlotte's parents are having a party at their place – anniversary I think. Anyway, they said Charlotte could invite a couple of people over. I was already here but she wanted to invite you too."

"I dunno…I kinda thought you two wanted some, you know…time alone…together. I don't wanna get in the way."

Deep down I knew that Charlotte had literally waited her entire life to be with Josh and now that *that* part of the timeline had been changed in her favour I wanted to let both of them get the most out of it without me being in the way.

"What? Oh don't be so soft. If we didn't want you around I wouldn't have called. Trust me, it's cool. I've asked Mum and she said it's fine as long as we're back by half ten at the latest. So quit wasting the batteries on my walkman and get over here!"

"Well, when you put it *that* way, how can I refuse?"

"Great! Devonshire Road, number…err…oh, it's the pebble-dashed one with the blue door and window boxes."

Devonshire Road. It rang a bell and I vaguely knew where it was. I knew it had a primary school somewhere along it and that it was a turn-off from the main road from Sutton and Belmont, so if I walked past Sutton train station along Brighton Road I was certain I'd come to it soon enough.

"Okay, if I can't find it I'll text you." I said, only realising my mistake when it was too late.

"You'll what?"

"Never mind, I'll be there soon, okay?"

"Cool. Bye then."

"Bye Josh."

*   *   *

I suppose I could have drifted through the back streets from Linda's house but I wasn't overly familiar with this part of Sutton and certainly not from this time period. Grandma and Grandpa had always lived in Cheam, which is a village next to Sutton, in all the time I'd lived with them. So whilst knowing Sutton High Street and the railway station I wasn't that clued-up on the backstreets. So with that in mind I made my way into town – becoming caught up in the commuter crowd the nearer I got.

Maybe it was the fact that the crowd were moving like an ocean tide that made that solitary figure standing outside the station so visible. It was Dad – looking worn-down as he stood watching the world go by and from his clothing it was clear he was on his way home from work. The look in his eyes was hauntingly familiar – it was the same one I often saw in my own reflection – a lost, longing gaze that screamed out for clarity. Did he know about Angie and that other man? Was *that* why he looked so beleaguered? Was *this* how it all started?

I knew Josh and Charlotte were expecting me but I couldn't leave Dad in that state. There had to be something, however small, that I could do to make him feel better and so with that in mind I made my way over to him – navigating through the tidal crowds; determined to make a difference.

"Dad…" I uttered instinctually as I got closer.

He didn't turn round and it took a second to realise why. He didn't know me here – not properly anyway, not as his son; so I had to play along by the rules of this place. "When in Rome…" and all that.

"James," I said, tapping Dad on the shoulder.

"Luke, hey, I didn't see you there. How are you?"

"Ok I guess. How about you?"

"Ha! How long've you got!" James answered absently.

His tone made it clear that he had a lot going through his mind and his use of humour emphasised the psychological mask he wore to the outside world. But he didn't need to do that – not with me. I understood, I really did. If only he'd let me in.

"Long enough." I replied.

James looked at me – gazing intently behind my eyes – as if looking inside me somehow, leaving me with the impression that he was sensing the true father-son relationship between us even if he didn't consciously realise it. This was his chance to reach out. I was here and willing to listen, if only he'd let down his guard.

"It's weird," he uttered eventually, "it's like I can tell you things I wouldn't tell anyone else."

"You can. I want to help."

"I...don't know. I mean, I don't wanna burden you – you're young, you should be enjoying yourself and getting into trouble or something, not listening to some failed graphic designer confessing his troubles."

"You're *not* a failure, James. Don't say that. You're a good guy. And as for burdening me, you're not. I wouldn't ask if I didn't want to know."

"Good guy, huh?! Try telling that to Angie." He replied absently.

At once the hairs on the back of my neck rose to attention as the chilling thought that Angie had already delivered her bombshell ran down my spine, leaving me wondering whether I was too late to substantially change anything. Had I missed my chance?

"Angie...what – what do you mean?"

"She's changing, Luke. My sweet little Angie is slipping away and I don't know how to fix it. I love her, Luke, I really do. At first I thought it was just postnatal depression but she's not bonding with Luke and lately it's been clear that something's very wrong – she's changed – more distant, like her life's calling her in a different direction; away from us. All I want is for her, me and little Luke to be a family but it's like her heart's not in it. I'm scared she's gonna leave me and him. What could I do if that happens?"

Listening to James' words, I wanted to indulge my gut-instinct and tell him to batten-down the hatches in preparation for that very outcome but somehow I knew that that level of honesty would break James' heart right now and so I searched for something to say that would help him and yet not provide false hope at the same time.

And even though the rush hour crowd was flowing past us at speed, James and I remained on the wall by the bus stop outside the station and talked through what was on his mind. It amazed me just how much he truly loved Angie, and soured my view of her even more now that I knew what she was doing behind Dad's back. It was so clear now – it made sense as to just how devastating Angie leaving James had been; if what he was saying now was any indication then when she left (in the original timeline) it had understandably forced James to retreat further into himself – an act that in turn was the catalyst for his self-imposed isolation over the years. How could she do this to him? I just couldn't understand and it seemed the more I learned about Angie the more of a stranger she became. All throughout, I tried boosting James' confidence – he was going to need it and that aside, he genuinely didn't deserve to be dealt the blow he had been. But as angry as I was with Angie I knew that Dad wouldn't be left alone to face things this time – I was here and determined to see him through this.

"Look, Angie being around or not doesn't stop you being a good parent and role model for your son."

"I don't know. He needs…he *deserves* both parents and I'm not convinced I can be who and what he needs."

"But you *can*, James. What he *needs* is a caring and supportive environment."

"I don't even know if I can provide *that*." sighed James heavily, "But more than anything, I don't want to be a disappointment to him. I couldn't bear seeing that look in his eyes. I'd rather stay away and not taint him with my failings. He *deserves* better than that; better than *me*."

The more we spoke the harder it was to fight tears from forming in my eyes. I'd never seen Dad like this – never understood him like this. It was like I could now see some deep similarities between the two of us and in many ways it was like trying to talk to the wounded parts of myself.

"James, Luke *deserves* his father…*and* his mother but if Angie truly doesn't want to be involved then he'll need you even more. Distancing yourself won't solve the problem, in fact if anything it'll make it worse. Imagine it from his perspective growing up seeing his father remaining distant. He'll begin blaming himself, thinking that somehow he's not good enough for either parent to want him. And he'll grow up angry and cold. Is that really what you want for him? Is that what you want for your little boy?"

"No, of course not but…that wouldn't be…I mean, of course he's good enough. He's perfect. I just wouldn't want to bring him down with my failings. I can't be perfect for him, even more so if Angie left, and that's what gets to me."

"You don't have to be perfect. Just be his father, that'll be more than enough for him. Trust me. Don't give up on him or yourself for that matter. You're *not* a failure, at anything, and I know you *really* love Angie but ultimately her decisions are hers to make and be responsible for. You're a good man, James Hudson, and a good father. Never lose sight of that. Luke *is* and *will be* proud of you, just as you are of him, take it from me."

By this point James seemed to have gained some measure of confidence as his posture seemed straighter and altogether more confident. I had done it. I had begun changing the timeline for the better. Things were far from over but at least I was making progress with James – instilling fresh confidence in him would theoretically decrease the chance of him falling as low as he did originally when everything kicks off.

"Thanks Luke. You've really helped, honestly. *Your* parents must be really proud to have a son like you, huh?"

"Well, fifty-percent." I answered candidly.

"Then the other fifty clearly doesn't know their arse from their elbow. Anyway, look…that's my bus so I'd best be off. I need to collect Luke from the childminder anyway – it's nearly tea-time. I'd best be off but…thanks again."

"No problem. Take care James."

He smiled before turning to join the small queue for the bus and I stayed back to watch him, returning his discreet wave when he eventually boarded the bus and found a window seat. I really *was* proud that he was my Dad. I'd learnt so much about him whilst being here that I understood why he'd behaved how he had done where I'd come from; he hadn't distanced himself because he was disappointed with *me*, he'd done it because he'd been disappointed with *himself*. James wanted above all else to be an exemplary parent and circumstances beyond his control had tainted and sapped his confidence to the extent where'd fallen into a dark place but God-willing that was going to change. James *would* get his chance to be the exemplary father he so wanted to be. I'd make sure of it.

*   *   *

It didn't take too long after that to find Charlotte's street and house. Using Josh's brief description, I located a house that fit the criteria and knocked on the blue wooden door, becoming instantly relieved when it opened to reveal Charlotte smiling back at me.

"Hey, there you are. Come in. We were beginning to wonder what happened to you. Is everything okay?"

"Yeah," I replied, "I think so. I ran into my Dad and we got talking. How about you – how's it going?"

"Great! It's been so good being with Josh, you know – *'officially'*. You don't know how much it means. Thank you so much for what you did." replied Charlotte, putting her arms around me.

"Hey," I said modestly, "it was always *supposed* to happen; I just gave it a nudge in the direction. You two are great together, congratulations."

"Thank you, now come on through, we've been waiting for you."

Charlotte led me through to the living room where a small selection of guests had gathered and were immersed in the feel-good vibe of the party – with the Hi-Fi churning out a lively blend of late-Seventies and Eighties music. I was introduced to Charlotte's parents, Sheila and Roger, and wished them a happy anniversary before finding Josh, who was busy working his way through a large glass of cola.

"So you made it then." He ribbed.

"Better late than never." I replied.

The party was great and even though I only really knew Josh and Charlotte, Charlotte's mum Sheila made everyone including myself feel welcome with her warm smile and infectious humour. To be honest, a lot of the music seemed new to me, which was ironic seeing as *it* was older than *I* was, but even so the atmosphere remained warm and jovial, with everyone contributing to the high spirits – making the evening a hearty celebration of love and togetherness.

Apart from anything else, seeing Josh and Charlotte so happy was great as well. They just seemed to go well together – one of those couples that looked set to be paired for life – soul mates, I suppose; and as they slow-danced to a series of romantic ballads Charlotte laid her head on Josh's right shoulder as they swayed in time to the rhythm while Josh cradled her as if holding a bride at the first dance after a wedding.

I was glad to have been invited. Things had been so chaotic lately that to just have some down-time was a blessing laced with gold. Here, now, for the briefest of reprieves the problems I had to overcome had been left on the other side of Charlotte's front door, allowing me the space to breathe and recharge as the evening passed slowly by. For that brief moment in time I was free to truly be myself among two of the best friends I'd come to know.

Chapter Nine

A while passed before I saw Angie again after discovering her infidelity. Though just about controlling my temper, I couldn't comprehend why she would do that to Dad...or me. Until now, even after Saturday, I'd clung onto the naive hope that Angie could be saved from her own selfish actions but fate, it seemed, was desperate to convince me otherwise. It was only by chance that I saw her again one evening after school on my way back home from *Artie's* – there she was, in a restaurant a few shops down from Sutton train station, getting intimate with the same guy from the other day. Here they were, living their secret life in full-view of the world and I don't know whether it was the fact of what Angie was doing or just the casual way she was going about it that got under my skin more. Now, like the other night and as before, there was more than a window pane separating us – once again there was a distance between us; once again I was stranger on the outside.

Even as she laughed at something her fancy man said to her I was partially spellbound by her presence. She was (at least supposed to be) my Mum – half of my heritage and yet there didn't seem to be anything other than blood connecting us. As I continued watching the two lovers interact across the dinner table I looked intently towards Angie in the hopes I'd recognise something, anything that would provide a near-tangible link I could build upon with her. But as she continued sitting there, looking like an extra out of *Dallas* with her frizzy "lion's mane" permed hairdo and uber-Eighties designer two-tone white dress with black edging and slanted 'V' belt, I couldn't help but succumb to the realisation that she was just too far out of reach.

Unable to contain my frustration I strode into the restaurant and stormed across to Angie's table like a gale-force hurricane – completely ignoring the protests of the uppity maitre-de in the process. Both Angie and her twenty-something yuppie fancy man looked up at me in bewilderment as I returned their glances with a glare that encapsulated all of the rage and heartache that was erupting inside. The man, dressed in a blue suit with white stripes that looked like pyjamas and reeking of some en-vogue cologne, poised himself to speak but fell short when met with the most resentful glare I've ever directed at anybody in my life.

"Out!" I ordered bluntly, motioning for him to leave.

He scoffed, momentarily taken aback and unsure how to respond.

"Angie, do you know this kid?" he asked eventually.

She nodded.

"Hey," I affirmed, "I *said* – out!"

He looked at Angie who reluctantly nodded before waving the maitre-de away and adding "Would you give us a moment?"

"Yah, for sure." He answered with a faint smile and discreet squeeze of her hand.

The yuppie Casanova drew his napkin up to the corners of his lips before discarding it on the table and getting up – staring at me with a look that could sour milk in the process. Inside I was screaming for him to give me some excuse...*any* excuse to knock him on his yuppie Thatcherite backside but instead, like two lions on the African plains we stood holding each other's gaze until at last he stepped past me and walked towards the entrance, withdrawing a packet of branded cigars from his pockets as he did so.

Quick as a flash I sat down and looked at Angie whilst filtering my rage into some semblance of a constructive conversation. Reaching for a breadstick and taking a bite, I continued glancing at Angie which was evidently unnerving her given her facial expression.

"Are you going to tell me what all this is about?" she demanded, sloshing the remaining red wine around in her goblet before taking a sip.

"Well," I began casually, "I was passing by when I saw the pair of you acting like a couple of lovesick teenagers and I thought 'hang on – that can't possibly be Angie in there flirting with that ten-a-penny yuppie sort because Angie is engaged to James, but low and behold – here you are. Do you care to tell me what *that* is about?!"

"Oh, Luke," she offered with a deceptively casual but thin smile, "Simon's just a friend from work."

"Really – if I treated *my* friends like that I'm pretty sure there'd be a restraining order heading my way."

"Whatever do you mean?"

"Do you French-kiss all your friends Angie, or is it just the ones you fancy?"

Her thin smiled quickly faded as she fiddled evasively with her frizzy permed-up hair.

"We were...*not* French-kissing."

"You were the other day – Saturday afternoon just off the High Street. Remember that?" I retorted.

Angie recoiled defensively as she realised that she couldn't lie her way out of this one. I wasn't about to let her off that easily.

"Oh my G-...are you spying on me? You know, there's a word for boys like you."

"Yeah, there's a couple of good'uns for *you* too." I sniped back.

She sat back, knocking back a mouthful of the red wine in her glass goblet as the mood between us dropped a few degrees below freezing.

"What are you doing Angie? What about James? What about your *son*?"

"Don't you *dare* talk to me like you know me. You don't know the first thing about me."

Like a calm sea stirring up into a raging torrent I saw a different side to Angie emerge like a formidable force of nature. That motivational power and charisma I'd seen her exhibit before so constructively now became fused to her anger like armour and drove her ever forward in her beliefs and convictions. Was this still the woman I'd met only a week or so ago? It didn't seem like it. *That* Angie had been every bit like the ideal I'd formed in my mind over the years; whereas *this* Angie was driven by repressed anger and unfulfilled desire – like a volcano waiting to erupt at a moment's notice. And I guess it was then that I realised who I'd inherited my temper from, as the volcano inside *me* began roaring into life.

"You're right – I *don't* know the first thing about you and there was a time when that hurt like hell but now...you know what, I'm *glad* because you're nothing but a disappointment." I seethed.

Quick as a flash, Angie swung her right palm at my face – landing a stinging slap straight upon my cheek before I could offer any resistance. For the briefest of moments we froze –

each caught in and by the mood before re-animating ourselves with Angie continuing to look upon me with a fallen fury while I cradled my stinging cheek.

"You wanna talk about disappointments, Luke? Huh? Let me tell you about disappointment. Disappointment is working towards a career and seeing everyone else living the high life while you're stuck on the bottom rung of the ladder on minimum wage; disappointment is waking up on the wrong side of twenty-five and realising you have nothing to show for your life; disappointment is feeling young and wanting to be free and then remembering the crushing responsibility that rests on your shoulders. I just want to escape all of that and be the person I feel like."

Duality rippled through me again like an unforgiving streak of lightning. Angie was clearly unhappy but I knew that her perception of 'escape' meant; I knew the trail of heartbreak and devastation it would leave as its legacy. Confused with the conflicting feelings coursing through me I struggled with what to say or how to react. I didn't know whether to feel sorry for or to be angry at her for being so selfish and self-absorbed. Was it possible to feel both at the same time?

"But you *have* a family – surely that's a reward as much as a responsibility."

Angie chuckled sarcastically – finding private humour in my plea as she sloshed the wine around again in her goblet and took another well-considered sip.

"Family wasn't *my* reward, Luke."

"What do you mean?"

"I never wanted a baby, okay – at least not for a long time – once I'd done what I wanted to do; but then I got pregnant and everything changed. I wanted to have an abortion but James pleaded with me to keep the baby. I love James – I really do but..."

"...but fooling around with strangers is more fun?!" I sniped, wounded by the implications of her words.

"Maybe," She replied absently, "Things are different now. James isn't the man I fell in love with anymore – he's changed. Even after Luke was born I knew I couldn't be a Mum – even then I suggested putting him up for adoption but James wouldn't hear of it – he kept on saying how we had a responsibility to bring Luke up right. Sometimes I think he loves that baby more than me."

"It's not a competition." I scowled.

"No, it's a nightmare," she replied, "But Simon changes all of that - we want the same things. It's like we just click, you know. He's so driven and he really connects with me."

"I don't care if he's *'the man from Del Monte'*, what you're doing is wrong. And the worst thing about it is that you *know* it's wrong and just don't care."

It was hard struggling to maintain my composure in light of what she'd said, with each of her words breaking another heartstring inside me and mercilessly tearing the dreams I'd held onto for so long asunder. What was harder was reconciling the fact that yes, Angie *was* my mother but at the same time she didn't want to be and apparently never had – and *that* hurt more than any slap to the face ever could.

My resolve must have faltered somewhat because Angie soon commented on the tears welling in front of my eyes.

"What have *you* got to cry about? It's not like I'm cheating on you. Besides, we're only family because of James."

And that was it - one cold singular moment of stark clarity. She had hit the nail right on the head.

"Yeah, you're right." I sneered, furious with her lack of remorse or feeling towards me or Dad, "Goodbye Angie."

With that I stormed out of the restaurant in the foulest of moods as the anger masked my wounded heart – and brushed passed her fancy-man Simon on the way out, not trusting myself to say a word to him – that was until *he* said something to me

"See you around kid. Perhaps you could ruin dinner for me another night, too."

As reason and logic flew fast from sight, I instinctually swung a punch at him – catching him off-guard and sending him stumbling a step and half back as I reached for one side of the collar of his long woollen coat. Fighting against both the urge to hit him again and the overpowering scent of his cologne, I pulled him closer and readied my parting shot.

"Listen to me you yuppie ponce – you may have Angie fooled with your sharp suit, cheap cologne and executive lifestyle but to me you're as transparent as that window. You can't even *begin* to imagine the hurt you and Angie are causing my family. Now, you may have her under your spell but I'm warning you – *this* is a line in the sand right here."

"Look, kid, I know the situation isn't ideal but I care about Angie, I really do. We're in love – when you're a little older perhaps you'll understand."

"Don't patronise me." I fumed.

"When you're in love you can't help which way you fall. Sometimes love can make rational people do irrational things. I never meant to hurt your family, neither did Angie but she's so unhappy at the minute and she has so much potential. I can show her the world. I can make her happy. Doesn't she deserve that?"

If it had been anyone else I think I'd of flat-out answered 'no' categorically but this was Angie we were talking about and as angry at her as I was for what she'd said and done, she was still my mother even she didn't want to be, and on some twisted level I still loved her.

"She does, but I don't agree with so many people being hurt by it. Look after her Simon. Make her happy. She's all yours."

Having said my peace and recovering from my flashpoint of rage, I left, not stopping until I was round the back of the railway station – next to the power substation situated just off Quadrant Way. It was raining lightly and getting dark as I slapped a wall with the palm of my hand in frustration – enduring the rough, stinging kiss it provided on my skin as the rain hid my tears. What was I going to do now? What could I do? Angie was a lost cause and moreover, did I even want to try keeping her around after what she'd said? Arguably, no. According to her, I, or rather younger version of me, was a large part of her feeling so trapped...so encumbered – why would she want to stay around if that was true? And all the while that single thought haunted me like a phantom – *"She doesn't want me. She never did"*.

*   *   *

The next day found me just as consumed by Angie's revelation as I had been last night, with even Auntie Linda's breakfast table banter failing to lift my spirits. I was so confused right now. My thoughts were all over the place. Conflicted. Uncertain. What she had said had cut deep – all this time I'd thought of her as a figure of hope when all along she'd regretted having me – that was a lot to take in and certainly not something I could bury or casually brush-off quickly.

School didn't make for much of a distraction either. For the most part it felt as if everyone was moving faster than me – moving a million miles a minute while I was living in slow motion – consumed by thought and circumstance. But things didn't stay in slow-motion for me for very long...

Third period was PE and tracksuit-clad Ms Phillips (emphasis on the silent 'z' in 'Ms') had the class playing football on the playing field round the back of the school. By some quirky twist of fate I'd managed to dodge the initial draft for the teams as myself and five others were benched as the first game got under way. There could have a zoological stampede run across the field for the attention I was paying as my thoughts were still in overdrive over what and how to change things between my parents. It *was* what I here for after all, and time was running out. Fast. What was I going to do now that Angie had shown her true colours and subsequently nailed them to the mast? She didn't want saving – she'd made that perfectly clear. I needed Grace. I *needed* answers but all I got was...

"Hudson, you're up, let's go."

It didn't even register that I was being called for until the shrill sound of Ms Phillip's whistle pierced the contemplative silence I'd immersed myself in – bringing my thoughts back to the playing field with the shattering burst of sound.

"Hudson, come on..."

Reluctantly I strode onto the field, passing the girl I'd been substituted for. Honestly, I couldn't be bothered with this – with everything else that was going on, *this* was an irritation. But I played along all the same, albeit begrudgingly. In truth I'd never much cared for football – basketball had always been *my* favourite. Unfortunately, Gary Collins and his two afterthoughts were also present and made sniping comments or menacing glances at me whenever we came into contact – to which I merely laughed (in pity). But then a short while later, as I went to pass the ball to a team-mate just shy of the box, it happened...

A sharp pain suddenly tore through my right ankle and I fell to the ground in a heap. It all happened so fast that largely it was a blur – that was until I saw Collins and his cronies smirking at me. He made no secret that it'd been him – with his mock celebrations being reciprocated by his two sidekicks. The bastard – *he'd* done this – probably in revenge for showing him up the other week. Damn, this ankle stung like hell and rolling my sock down to inspect the damage I saw a mass of pinkish-red skin, with particularly dark circular patterns in some places – depicting stud patterns from football boots.

Struggling to my feet, I bore the pain as best I could while walking over to him – with the scene quickly becoming like one of those showdowns you'd get in a Western, with both parties ready to open fire in the blink of an eye. And it wasn't just Collins and myself that were drawn into the moment either – some others had stopped playing to watch from a (somewhat safe) distance.

With Collins' cronies flanking him like mismatched furniture, I put all I could into one hard shove that ended up sending the bully tumbling onto his disrespectful backside. He was startled for a moment but quickly flew up back to his feet – refusing help from his entourage in the process. Suddenly I became momentarily paralysed by the surge of adrenaline electrifying my chest before being able to move again – just in time for Collins to come ploughing into me as the two of us stood with chest pressed against chest – ready to blow this thing up into all-out war.

"You've just made a big mistake." sneered Collins.

"Likewise."

And then came Phillips' whistle again – blasting across the pitch from where another game was simultaneously going on - blanketing everyone with its shrill demand for non-negotiable silence.

"Hudson, Collins," she said sternly, jogging up to us, "What the hell is going on?"

"Hudson came over and pushed me, Miss."

"It's true Miss, I saw."

"Me too."

Oh great! So now it was my word against three of them – marvellous! Nothing like equal competition. Somehow I got the sinking feeling that this wasn't going to work out in my favour and surprise, surprise, how right I was...

"Hudson, you're out of line. Apologise." proclaimed Phillips, with her hands commandingly hugging her hips.

"What?!" I exclaimed, "To *him*?! No way. *He* fouled *me* – deliberately."

"I didn't see that."

"Then you need your eyes tested lady because *that's* how it happened."

I was fuming and inside that familiar primal anger began stirring – the animal inside me was waking up and once again I was a slave to its potent embrace.

"How dare you?! Go get changed and report to Mrs Burridge at once."

At that, some of the surrounding spectators let out a feigned "*ohhh...*" in the wake of Phillips' uncompromising decree and in that instant I felt the familiar burning sensation of the judgemental eyes gazing upon me – watching, waiting, mocking. It didn't matter how many times I'd felt this or indeed been misjudged, every time cut just as deep as the last. And inside, that primal animal rallied a defensive and defiant battle-cry...

"You've made a big mistake," I said before turning to Collins and pointing a stern, judgemental finger, "And *you*...they'll be writing country music about how big a mistake *you've* just made."

"You're all talk." He sneered.

"Try me."

"That's enough," demanded Phillips, "Hudson – *GO!*"

And so, having been unceremoniously misjudged, tried and summarily dismissed without appeal, I stormed off the pitch as best I could with my ankle still throbbing – not bothering to look back as there was nothing worthwhile that I'd left behind. Again I became aware of the crushing multitude of everything that was going on and I didn't know what to focus on. That little spat with Collins had exhumed a torrent of suppressed anger and my mind became awash with fresh thoughts of Angie's betrayal; Dad's impending meltdown and Josh's endangered mortality flooding to the forefront. Not only hadn't I worked out what to do about *them*, but now I'd been played like an orchestra by Collin's calculating deviancy and *that* didn't sit well with me. Not one iota.

As it turned out Burridge was busy in some uninterruptable meeting, forcing her secretary to send me along to Mr Carson who, weirdly enough, was apparently my Head of Year. Small world or what?!

From the instant I knocked on the old wooden door to Carson's classroom he seemed to know why I was there – with his unseen yet all-seeing ability to look inside people. He was in the middle of teaching a class and so opened the door slightly, addressing me with a disarmingly neutral tone of voice.

"Mr Hudson, to what do I owe this unexpected surprise?"

"I...got kicked out of PE and Mrs Burridge was busy so they sent me to you."

"I see. Am I allowed to ask *why* you got kicked out of PE?"

"Collins. But it wasn't my fault, honestly. Not really. But...I got the blame."

Carson looked at me and I'm guessing he must have genuinely believed me because his tone remained the same – non-judgemental and mediating as he opened the door further.

"Okay, I tell you what we're gonna do – you can stay in here until lunchtime and continue working on that essay I set you. I expect it to be finished by the time the lunch bell rings, okay? Fair enough?"

"Yes sir."

"Right, I guess you'd better come in then. Sit at the back. Okay class....settle down. Where were we?"

Sitting at the back of the class I filtered out the sound of class and Carson's lesson as I put the pen and lined paper in front of me and stared at it – hoping it would tell me what to write. I knew why Carson had asked me to do this and I knew the therapeutic merit writing would offer but it hard to articulate the thoughts and feelings that had lurked inside my head and heart for so long. In doing so I'd have to confront them and that was the scary part – they were so strong and overwhelming – like that animalistic rage with me – that facing up to them much less overcoming them seemed a daunting challenge if ever there was one. But I knew I had to do it and so with a rush of confidence and uncertainty, I reached for the pen and began merging thought and feeling with language until something constructive began hitting the page...

When people ask me of my pain I say that it is a beast that rarely sleeps. Anger is often considered an expression of, or against, that which is repressed and it is further considered that repression can only occur when potent desires are ignored by the external environment. It's a pain that can split your soul in-two and precipitate the most violent of thunder storms in your heart. We are taught at an early age to conform – to follow and accept without question. But what if there are questions lurking inside – festering away like a contagion? What if those questions and desires are so deeply embedded within us that to deny them would be to deny the sun from rising? That is _my_ reality. That is _my_ pain.

Psychology shows us how influential people and experiences are to the developing individual – but what happens when those established forms are distorted – when rites of passage and baseline human desires such as affiliation, affection and esteem are marginalised by circumstance? Parents are important – they are the primary means by which a child learns social cognitive abilities. Parents condition their children how to respond and interact with the world and so an absence of that guidance can be understood to lead to atypical development.

My father, James, is a good man at heart but he is also haunted by issues from his own atypical childhood. It seems that that struggle has become endemic to our legacy. For years I've struggled with the parental paradox James embodies – he desires to be a good father and role-model and yet he withdraws physically and emotionally to the extent where he seems to largely exist on the fringes of my life – becoming a peripheral parent. For as long as I can remember I've been angry at him and myself because of this: at him because he possesses the power and opportunity to be involved in my life and yet chooses not to; and I get angry at myself because I feel that I am not worth his interaction – like there are elements to me he recognises and actively wants to distance himself from. Like somehow his withdrawal is my fault, like I'm an undesirable or unworthy son for him.

Of course, operating synergistically with this is the physical and emotional abandonment presented by Mum, Angie. She's never been involved in my life for reasons that had never been made clear to me until recently. She had always been a somewhat mythologized figure to me growing up – I used to pin all my hopes and aspirations for things to change upon her – believing that she could and would make everything alright just by being around. But, as I've learnt, the fissure between rhetoric and reality can often be greater than any one person can imagine. I got to meet her for the first time recently and was instantly spellbound by the hope that her presence could elicit all those desires I'd dreamed of throughout childhood – of finally being a unified and loving family. As it turns out, dreams can truly be shattered, as I found out that she hadn't wanted me but instead had opted to pursue her own dreams and ambitions instead of tending to her responsibilities. Am I truly that bad that neither parent wants to bother with me? Have I done something or become someone that's so far removed from what either of them wants? I just don't understand. It doesn't make sense and that's the frustrating thing. Without sense there is no reason and without reason there is nothing stable to strategise against or towards.

With James I can sort of understand why he's distant but Angie is different – she isn't haunted by the same ghosts Dad is. And yet she still makes the same decision to exclude herself from me. Why?

Where is reason and compassion? If all things are meant to have purpose then why is this matter seemingly so devoid of any substantial basis? Why can't things be different? I wish they could be.

Growing up I've seen the few people I allowed myself to get close to, sharing the collective warmth and strength that family is inherently supposed to provide and wondered why I was never allowed to have the same. I mean, I've been raised by my grandparents for as long as I can remember and they're lovely – they've really tried to make things normal for me over the years but no amount of substitute parenting can fill the gap left by my biological parents. I love my grandparents but so many times I've wished that my actual parents were around – to interact with me, recognise what I was doing, to tell me off when I did something wrong. I've seen my friends being recognised, accepted and loved by close family ties and wished beyond all reason that that could be me. It's like a vampiric addiction – the more you see it around you, the more you want it – with desire devolving into some twisted emotional bloodlust. It's hard to keep it all inside. One day I'm convinced the mask will crack and the world will see me for what

I am inside - broken and angry, and I hate that. It's so wrong.

This anger inside me, this venom I am left harbouring slowly poisons me - turning me cold, keeping me alone. When aroused by what it seeks but cannot possess it roars into life - becoming a primal animal within me, with anger so potent it feels as if it'll rip through my flesh and escape regardless of how much I endeavour to keep it in check. The beast becomes me - wearing me down and wearing me out until at last all my earthly faculties surrender to it - letting it roar with my voice and see with my eyes. The anger, the animal, becomes me no matter how much I don't want it to. And every time it happens that primal animal says that this will be the last time it has to roar, the last time that it has to fight. That this will be the fight to end all fights but that's never true. The cycle always continues - the beast wakes up, raises hell and slumbers again until the next time, leaving me to deal with the aftermath it leaves me with on each occasion. I become a slave to my emotions. It's poisonous and shaming but that is my reality. That is my pain.

I finished writing about fifteen minutes or so before the bell was scheduled to go off and spent the remainder of that time going over what I'd written – finding it hard to see the reasons for my anger staring back at me in a tangible black-and-white form. It was strange and slightly unnerving to have laid my soul bare on paper but was also surprisingly liberating to have released these poisonous thoughts from inside. It was truly a breakthrough to have named my demons and got them down on paper – *that* was half the battle.

When the bell eventually rang the class filed out like that stampede of wild animals in a film I vaguely remembered from childhood, until only Mr Carson and myself were left and as he made his way towards me I felt a sudden surge of strength and pride from within – that this essay was my tangible justification for what I felt – it was like a banner I could ride into with – showing the true colours of the cause I was embroiled in and now more than ever I was ready to show that to the world. Come what may. This was who I was and even though I didn't feel at peace with all of it, I wasn't about to let the shame silence me any longer. My voice would be heard.

"Have you finished?"

I nodded.

"May I see?"

I nodded again and slid the lined paper towards his side of the desk, allowing him to reach out for it and pick it up. He must have only been a couple of sentences in when his expression deepened and he pulled one of the nearby chairs over and sat down as he continued delving into the furore of my mind. Carson seemed winded by my words – as if they were far removed from what he had been expecting and potent enough to seem formidable even to him. Minutes passed like hours as he read the essay intently but the silence only served to strengthen my resolve – I'd harboured that pain for far too long and now, thanks to Mr Carson, other people could know the tragedy my lips dared not speak; they too could feel as I felt and understand the beast that sleeps inside my heart.

"Luke, I... had no idea." Carson uttered eventually.

"No-one does – that's what makes it hurt so bad. It should be so obvious. I mean, everyone *needs* parents, right?"

"Sure"

"So why don't mine want me? What's wrong with me? What did I do?"

I knew Carson couldn't answer those questions but even so that animalistic pain inside screamed those thoughts out anyway with my voice. Inside, as much as outside, I demanded answers and clarity.

"Luke, there's nothing wrong with you and *you* didn't do anything wrong. Whatever problems your parents have are *theirs*, not *yours*. Besides, from what you've written it seems like your Dad's keen to take an interest in you."

"Yeah but he cuts himself off a lot. He won't let himself get close to me and I don't know *how* to get close to *him*."

"Maybe he's hurting too, in his own way. *Perhaps* he feels just as imperfect as a father as you feel as a son. Perhaps the two of you are more alike than you realise. Life's not easy,

Luke, and it doesn't come with an instruction manual. Sometimes people just have to muddle through as best they can. You have to fight for the ones you care about in life."

And then it hit me. A sudden lightning flash of clarity and realisation. Putting together what Carson and Grace had said finally made the pieces slot into place enough for me to see a majority of the picture. I wasn't here to keep my parents together - I never had been. In my head I'd let that perfect ideal take over and shape what I thought I had to do but I'd been wrong and now that fog was clearing. *Now* I realised what Grace had meant by major changes needing a sacrifice. Angie was destined to leave Dad and nothing I could do could change that. I *had* to save Dad. I was *here* to save Dad. *That* was the sacrifice. I'd been right before – I had to lose one parent to save the other one. Angie may have walked out but Dad had stayed – even in the screwed-up future I'd come from. For all his faults he still *wanted* to be there for me, to be there with me. And knowing that, I wasn't about to give up on him. Carson was right – you had to fight for the ones you love and I was going to do just that. James Hudson *would* get the chance to be a fantastic father; and we *would* get the chance to be a family. Destiny had led me to this moment and now I understood what had to be done.

Chapter Ten

A few days later Josh and I were walking home from school – each recounting our days to one another – sharing stories of humorous occurrences and eccentric teachers. It had been a good day actually although *anything* would have easily been an improvement on the other day. Since then, and the now infamous football pitch incident, Collins and his cronies were keeping their distance with every minor encounter in the corridors or grounds of the school becoming like a clichéd high-noon showdown from one of those Western movies Grandpa always lovingly watched.

Meanwhile, the blossoming romance between Charlotte and Josh was going from strength to strength with Charlotte living in every moment they spent together and Josh going out of his way to be chivalrous by opening doors, pulling out seats and extended Charlotte every courtesy he could imagine. Things had reached an exceptionally tranquil counterpoint lately but as good as things were I was aware that they were due to step up a gear soon. Time was steadily catching up to us.

On the way home Josh and I stopped in the park next to the High Street, where he set about retrieving a time-worn leather football from his rucksack. With the weather remaining cheerily optimistic, the two of us began playing a one-on-one game – discarding our jumpers and ties and using them in conjunction with our bags as makeshift goalposts. Having the marriage of time and circumstance to enjoy a spontaneous moment like this was truly beyond compare. In adulthood, moments like this become like some secular Grail – small fragments of life when nothing else matters but for the wholesome enjoyment of life itself. Growing up there hadn't really been many relatives (that I either knew of or lived near) that I could have moments like this with. Even with the few friends I allowed myself to get close to, moments like this hadn't been commonplace – with our individual angst and sense of isolation from the mainstream drawing us together to the extent where we existed as outsiders from the "norm" – on the outside looking in instead of the other way round. In any event, playing football with Josh was as refreshing as the cool breeze that swept through the stalwart trees and across the sun-kissed park. A fair way into the game Josh kicked the ball far out of play and I jogged across the grass to retrieve the ball and back again.

"Where's Charlotte?" I asked while trying to swirl the ball around on one finger like a basketball.

"At the café I think."

"Wanna stop by before heading home?"

"Nah, Charlotte asked me not to."

"What?! Why?" I asked, confused.

"She said she needed to talk to Grace about something important – alone."

From what little he had said it was clear Charlotte had stumbled across something important surrounding the accident Josh was destined to endure in this timeline. But what? I *had* to know more. I *wanted* to know more. I wanted to do everything I could to make sure it didn't happen.

"Did she say what it was about?" I enquired causally.

"No, not really. We were talking earlier and then all of a sudden she got all serious like a switch had been flicked on in her head. Anyone would have thought it was a matter of life and death."

I smiled as I fought to contain the shimmering sensation of goosebumps breaking out across my forearms. Clearly something Josh had said to Charlotte earlier had related to how...*it*...had happened and now she was primed like a warhead – determined with every fibre of her being to put things right for the one her head and heart had fallen for. I really wanted to be there – helping in any way I could but I knew that sticking with Josh was the right thing to do. Until I caught up with Charlotte it was probably best I kept a close eye on Josh just in case "*it*" was due to happen sooner than she could tell me.

"It's probably just girl stuff, don't worry about it. Call her later; I'm sure it'll be cool." I lied dismissively, "C'mon, bet I can beat you in *'best out of three'*. What do you say; first one to get three goals buys the other one a drink on the way home?"

"Go on then. Better get your money ready, pal." Josh smiled.

"Bring it on!"

And so, having diffused any tension, the two of us resumed the game – both just enjoying the moment and the carefree moment of youthful enjoyment – determined that, for the moment at least, the world and its worries remain on the other side of the iron park gates and perimeter railings.

*   *   *

When we did eventually arrive home some time around five, Linda was sitting at the kitchen table – looking as if she had the weight of the world on her shoulders. Josh, quite innocently, remained completely oblivious to the worn expression that clung to Linda's face as he raided the fridge for a cold drink.

"Hey Mum,"

"Hi Josh, Hi Luke. Have you boys had a good day?" she asked as she cradled a coffee cup with both hands.

"I was alright I guess. Is it okay to watch the TV for a bit?"

"Yes but *don't* forget your homework."

"I won't, I won't," came the absent reply as Josh made a b-line for the living room, with a glass of fresh orange juice in hand.

"Hey, Auntie Linda, is everything okay?" I asked after Josh had disappeared.

She looked up, noticeably surprised that I hadn't joined Josh, and a thin smile momentarily shone through her otherwise troubled expression.

"It will be sweetheart, it will be. Things are just a bit difficult right now."

"How come?"

"James is going through a rough patch and I don't know how to help him." She shared before hushing her tone despite only us two being within earshot, "Angie's left him and little Luke – says she's fallen in love with some guy from work and wants 'other things'. James is devastated. I just can't believe Angie would do this to him. I've always said she was no good for him. The only good thing to ever come out of that relationship is little Luke, bless him."

There were no words to describe how I felt at that moment. In an instant – BANG – that tranquillity that I had savoured for the past couple of weeks been unceremoniously shattered with the coming of the moment I'd been bracing myself for since arriving here. *This* was when it happens. I needed to act *fast; now*. And even though I still felt some (albeit limited) connection to Angie I could neither dispute nor get angry at what Linda was saying about her. Whatever Angie's motives, her actions will and would hurt a lot of people, with her happiness coming at the expense of any other, myself included and somehow, despite wanting to be fair towards her, I simply couldn't reconcile that.

"I just got off the phone to him before you boys got home. He's not in a good way. It sounded like all hell was breaking loose over there. He said she's packing up her stuff ready to move out tonight. I want to be there for him but I don't know what help I'd be – if I went there I know I'd end up in a slanging match with that woman. I just...I mean, *how* could she just walk out James and her own son?"

"I'll go." I announced resolvedly.

"What?"

"I'll go. *Someone* has to be there with him."

"Oh, sweetheart, that's very sweet but...no...I couldn't ask that of you."

"You're not. I'm volunteering. James needs family around him right now. I'll go. I'll make sure he's alright." I affirmed adamantly.

Linda looked over at me as if poised to answer but no sound came. The unspoken sentiment in our expressions and shared words said all that needed be said and in that instant it was decided. Part of me felt uneasy leaving Josh alone In light of Charlotte as-yet unknown discovery but still, he *was* at home and *I'd* been brought back to 1990 for the very reason that had now surfaced between my parents. I *needed* to do this. I *had* to make a difference. The time was *now*.

I didn't even stop to change into something casual – I simply left my bag discarded on the side and rushed my door-key lanyard into one of my trouser pockets before promising to call Linda later with an update and leaving the house with all the force of a twister ripping through anything in its path. The roads and street-names became a blur, blending seamlessly into one another as I hurried to my parents flat, following the route Uncle Henry had taken the other week as if on autopilot while my mind continued churning over what I'd find there and how I could help Dad get over the loss of the woman he'd devoted his heart to. What would I do? What would I say? Would this be the last time I ever saw my mum before she forever became "Angie" – the stranger and shadow of my origin?

Arriving at the block of flats a short while later I saw a metallic blue Ford Sierra Sapphire parked outside with the engine running and hazard lights blinking. From the extras on the bodywork and the plush look of the interior, it was the type of car that made a statement about a person's status – like some mechanical phallus. As I stepped closer I saw a familiar figure waiting impatiently in the driver's seat; a man with slicked-back, gelled hair and blue pinstripe suit that was outmatched only by the striking pungency of his overpowering aftershave.

"Well, you certainly get around, don't 'cha?" he said, poking his head out the window after spying me in the wing mirror.

It was Simon in all his yuppie-ness: sharp suit, red braces, irritatingly smug grin and enough cologne to make even a Great White turn and run a mile in the opposite direction. Why was I not surprised that wherever there were problems between my parents, this guy was lurking like the archetypal uninvited guest somewhere in the immediate background?

"As do you, Simon, I could smell you half a block away. I don't suppose you care about the people you're hurting by doing this, huh? I don't suppose it evens registers with you that up there, right now, there's a guy about to lose the woman he loves and a baby about to lose his mother. Do you even have a conscience, Simon? Do you even know what the word means?"

I was fuming. Beyond fuming in fact. Mum was leaving Dad, *and* me, for this...caricature of 'success'. In that moment, I was overwhelmed by the temptation to yank those red braces of his and loop them around his scrawny, nonchalant neck; but I knew I had to *try* and keep a level head about all this – getting overly angry wouldn't make me of any use to helping Dad.

"Look, kid," Simon uttered condescendingly, "Here's a little 'Blue Sky Thinking' for ya...Angie and I aren't the first couple to be in this situation and we won't be the last. These things happen; that's life. Besides, I'm the one Angie wants."

"I couldn't give two brass ones if you're the 'Man from Del-Monte', you don't even *begin* to compare with the man she's leaving up there. People like you are *everything* that is wrong with this world."

Simon laughed under his breath, remaining cool and composed throughout; shocking me with his blatant detachment and disregard, genuinely not caring as if the pain his actions were and would be causing didn't even faze him in the slightest.

"You got spirit, kid. I'll give you that." he answered with mild humour and further disregard.

And so as I walked away before my temper hit the point of no-return I took the door-key from my pocket and dug it into the paintwork along the length of the car – creating a deep, noticeable wound along the otherwise pristine metallic blue paintwork; and prompting Simon to almost jump out of the driver-side door in response.

"Hey," he called after me, "this car cost more than your education! What the hell have you done? This'll cost a fortune to re-spray."

And it was with an unseen yet wry and darkly satisfying grin that I answered him as I continued towards the entrance to the block – never turning back once to face him.

"What a shame. But these things happen Simon; that's life."

And leaving a distraught Simon nursing his wounded phallus, I breezed into the brick-built block of flats and made my way up the three flights of stairs, all the while the adrenaline charged through me with all the power of an electricity sub-station.

Reaching the third floor it was immediately evident what was going on as a small gathering of black bin-bags and small boxes littered the enclosed corridor outside my parent's flat; with the eclectic assortment stealing the focus away from the beleaguered large potted communal cheese-plant and bleak chequered carpet tiles. Negotiating my way across the small minefield of move-out debris I neared the front door, finding it ajar and stopped at the sight of Angie opening it, bringing out a medium-sized suitcase adorned with some ghastly imitation almost-floral design. She looked troubled, upset and a shadow of the woman I'd begun to know. Angie was wearing a baggy, blue, shapeless jumper, black leggings and white slip-on shoes. Upon seeing me she stopped and observed me with a glance that screamed her guilt from every outlet of expression.

"I...don't want to hurt them...either of them." She uttered eventually.

"You've sure got a funny way of showing it."

It was the strangest thing but as we stood there in that moment I could neither forgive nor hate her. She was flawed but she was still my Mum and I found it hard to reconcile the twisted blend of anger and compassion inside me for her.

"I wish I could explain it. Please, don't judge me too harshly."

"Just...*go*." I sighed, not wanting her to but knowing she would.

I didn't want to fight her. I didn't want to hate her, but equally I couldn't pretend that I was alright with what she was doing either. And so with that Angie stepped past me, scooped up the small assortment of bags and boxes and walked away without another word being said between us; pre-empting a silent goodbye to be shared between the two of us as the mystery of how and why Angie had walked out of my life was finally answered. Fragments of my innocence and childhood dreams faded with her as she descended the stairs until at last there was only the faint echo of her shoes tapping against the step-guards and the faint scent of her fruity perfume lingering in the air. She was gone. *She* was Angie.

It took a moment to pull my own head together before I could even contemplate going inside to support Dad. Leaning against the exterior window in the corridor I could see Angie and Simon packing the last few things into the boot of the car, with Simon consoling a clearly conflicted Angie. A thousand things ran through my mind; a thousand things I wanted to say to her; a thousand things that remained unsaid – she'd made her choice, and now people like me and Dad were going to have to deal with the aftershock. Again, I wanted to hate her, to solidify my anger into a single targeted response but I couldn't hate her; as twisted as it sounded I *still* felt something for her, something that prevented me from demonising her. Damn, this was hard. This was one of the hardest things I'd ever had to face.

Stepping across the threshold the striking potency of the atmosphere inside was unashamedly apparent – with every wall and doorway appearing as heavy as I imagined James' heart to be right now. Closing the front door, I prepared myself for the fallen incarnation of James that awaited me as 80s new wave music echoed from the living room. New Wave had always been Dad's favourite type of music, certainly as long as I'd known him; I guess it reminded him of a time before adulthood cheated him of his innocence.

In the living room, Dad sat on the floor – a solitary figure with his back against the wall and his left arm shielding his weeping eyes. Amidst a chaotic mess of broken items that silently spoke of a scarring battle and all at once my frustration at Angie intensified as I was forced to endure the sorrowing sight of my broken father. How could she have left someone who loved her as much as James did? How could she have walked out and left him like this – so fractured and unhappy? Why did her pursuit of happiness have to rip Dad apart like this? It just wasn't fair.

"Hey," I mustered meekly.

Dad looked up, wiping the tears from under his glasses as his fallen expression softened slightly.

"Luke, what...what are you doing here?"

"I...wanted to be here so...you're not on your own."

His expression softened further.

"Thank you."

Negotiating through the debris I sat down next to him- far enough to give him the space he needed but close enough to show him he wasn't on his own. It suddenly became hyper evident that *everything* I did and said now would impact upon changing the timeline. *This* was when and how I had to save Dad. *Everything* was significant.

"Never fall in love, Luke. It hurts too much when it goes wrong." James offered with a sigh.

"Hey, you can't close yourself off from the rest of the world. If you do you'll only be punishing yourself. Trust me. I once went out with this girl, Hayley, who I liked, and I mean *really* liked – I'd have done anything for her."

"What happened?"

"I screwed it up. I didn't mean to but I did; I closed myself off because of other things that had happened and didn't want to let anyone get close to me because I didn't want to get hurt. But in the end it hurt me more because I pushed Hayley away."

"Young love, eh!" James grinned sympathetically.

"Love in general, Dad....I mean...'dad-e-o'." I replied, initially embarrassed by my mistake and then cringing at my lame attempt to recover the situation.

Thankfully James was momentarily lost in thought, turning to face me briefly – studying me with a curious expression before returning his focus on the far wall. Something in that look signified some unspoken resonance of the father-son connection between us. Even if Dad didn't realise it, part of him, somewhere inside, felt and trusted that link. I truly was his son, surprised that we were alike in so many respects – thoughts, motivations, fears. I had made similar mistakes with Hayley as Dad had made with me and the rest of the world.

"You know, it always feels like you've lived more of a life than you could have. You're fifteen and you talk as if you're more like twenty-five." James said casually.

"Age is only skin deep, James. But look – the point I'm trying to make is not to let that pain define you."

"But it hurts so much. I felt so complete with Angie. Before Luke came along it was like me and Angie against the world and then when he was born it was like I finally had a family I could look after and love. Don't get me wrong, I love Mum, Dad and Linda and so on but its different when you start your own family; and when you're brought into one. With Luke there's a connection that I don't remember experiencing with my Dad. It's different somehow…maybe it's because that biological link is there with Luke that isn't with Dad, I don't know. And Angie...*woah*...she's so motivated. When we met it was like the stars had conspired to bring us together, you know. She was haunted by a few things as we all are but to me she was perfect, she was my Angie – sharp-tongued and quick witted. I know why this has happened...you see; her parents always pushed her, perhaps too far. When we first met she was desperate to escape the cycle of having to bust a gut just to get some measure of their approval. She was angry at her family and I felt detached from mine – it's what united us at first – we were kindred spirits."

"No-one's doubting your commitment to Angie. But she's made her choice, James, and you deserve to live life outside of the shadow she's cast."

"I still love her."

"I know you do. I know. And honestly, I understand but you can't let this stop you from being the great person *and* father that you are. It's painful now but it'll get better; *you'll* get better."

"What about little Luke?"

"He'll understand in time. But he *needs* his Dad, *now* more than ever." I affirmed as the new wave music echoed throughout the room.

"Yeah...I guess you're right. I just hope I can be what he needs."

"You will be, just give it time."

The unspoken connection between us right now was positively electric. I understood Dad so much better now and respected him for his unseen strength of heart and mind. And it kept on surprising me just how alike we were as he went on to articulate thoughts and fears that I'd harboured silently for years, believing them to be a problem I had but here he was – sharing the same anxieties and preoccupations I'd been troubled by. Even now at his lowest point James had my complete respect and I was brimming with pride that he and I were father and son – a far-cry from the feelings I'd had towards him before arriving in 1990.

After a little while I made us both a cuppa as Dad continued reminiscing – seemingly gaining some measure of inner strength from fond memories – looking backwards in order to go forward.

"Ah, what do I do, eh Luke?"

"What do you mean?"

"All this...*today*...it's woken me up. I was putting up with things before even though they were making me unhappy but I want that to change. *I* wanna be the one in charge of my world, not Angie and certainly not that crappy job I'm stuck in. Things need to change. *I* need to change. I have to be at my best if I'm gonna be able to do the best for myself and my son."

"So change your job – even be your own boss. It's possible."

"Pfft! What could I do? I have about 4 O levels to my name. No secure, well-paying job is gonna look at me twice these days. Besides, it's all moving towards computers nowadays and I have no idea when it comes to those things – hell, I have to fight with the microwave just to set the bloody clock."

I couldn't help mustering a small laugh. Dad really didn't like technology, so much so that in the time I came from he'd actively go out of his way to avoid using it – preferring to queue up in a bank to pay his bills rather than arranging direct debits and even handwriting letters to friends instead of emailing or texting them. In a strange, unknown kind of way I really respected him for that. It was one of his quirks that set him apart from the crowd.

"How about graphic design – I know you like it and you've got a real talent for it. There's night school or college. It'll be worth doing a course if you wanna make a career out of it. Besides, it's important to do something you care about or else what's the point?"

Dad mulled the idea over for a few seconds before speaking again.

"D'you really think I could do it, for a career I mean? Wouldn't I be too old for night school or college?"

"Of course you could do it and no-one's too old to better themselves. If it's something that's important to you then go for it. Trust me – the stuff in that brown leather portfolio of yours will get you through the door of any self-respecting art and design college."

"How...how do you know about that? I hardly show it to anyone."

Over the years I'd snuck several peeks at Dad's portfolio in a bid to try understanding him better through his art. To anyone who'd seen his work it was no secret that what his lips couldn't confess to living company his hands could confess to a sketchpad. Certain sketches of Dad's had stuck out over the years – the two hands (with ID bracelets dangling from the wrists – one saying "James" and the other "Angie") emerging from opposite corners of the page trying to meet in the middle but stopped by a large lightning bolt entitled "fate"; a man who's parachute wouldn't open as he plummeted declaring "next time I'm taking the bus"; and a beautifully detailed family portrait of Grandma, Grandpa, Dad and Auntie Linda, with everyone except Dad coloured in. Of course, I couldn't tell him the truth so, conjuring up a feasible excuse, I turned to him to reply.

"I...saw it the other week when I was babysitting. You should really do something with that talent, James; it'd be a waste not to."

I *knew* it was something he wanted and something that, where I'd come from, he'd spent years regretting not having pursued – growing progressively more disenchanted with the string of unsatisfying jobs he'd endured by 2010. I was reacquainting him with one of his dreams and it was clear from the electric twinkle in his eyes that it was a dream he was still ever-keen to embrace. To me, Dad's road to recovery started with ambition and I was going to resurrect his.

A sudden cry from one of the bedrooms prompted James to get up, grabbing his acoustic guitar as he hurried out of the room. I followed close behind – lingering in the doorway as James adjusted the blanket the crib before softly strumming the intro to "*Johnny and Mary*". As I listened in it finally dawned on me how and why this song meant so much to Dad – with the lyrics being equally as applicable to Dad and Angie as they are to the characters in the song – with Angie never understanding Dad and Dad struggling to make sense of the world he found himself lost in.

I knew that it was going to be a rocky road in the day and weeks to come but all the while I was in 1990 I was adamant I'd move Heaven and Earth to help get over Angie and get on with his life. Dad needed to adapt to life as a single parent; he needed to find his way in life and I believed that he could do just that. Before coming to 1990 I always thought Dad went out of his way to avoid me and yet when it had mattered, Dad had been there for me and now that *he* needed someone, I was doing all I could to help him anyway I could because that's what families do – that is the kind of family I was here fighting for. I was determined to make things turn out alright come what may.

"It's just us two now son but we're gonna be alright." James said quietly to the now slumbering infant.

Frozen, I looked on silently as if watching a memory on playback.

"We are <u>now</u>." I thought.

Chapter Eleven

The following morning I finally got the chance to catch up with Charlotte properly when Josh stopped off at a newsagent to buy a cold drink. All the way there Charlotte kept quiet – opting instead to carefully observe Josh's every move and hanging longingly on every word. Bless her; she was love-struck and desperate for fate not to take him as it had done the first time around. She held faithfully onto his arm all the way – never letting him out of here reach for an instant. It was clear just how much she loved him and heart-wrenching to see the pain welling behind her gaze – her silent torment at knowing what was to be if nothing could be done. In a way I knew how she felt – it was the same, sort of, with Dad – I knew how he'd turn out if I didn't intervene and so I leapt at every chance I got to make things better. In life, if you truly care for someone, you'd do anything within your power to make sure they were alright.

Reluctantly Charlotte let go of Josh's arm as he walked into the newsagents, leaving the pair of us waiting outside.

"So how'd it go with Grace?" I asked.

"What? How...how do you know about that?"

She was on edge – as if she hadn't relaxed or even slept properly in a short while – hiding her deep-seated distraction under the veil of a thin smile.

"Relax – I just wanna help."

Charlotte sighed.

"I know...sorry. I thought I'd be ready for this but I'm so scared."

She looked close to tears, having been worked up into a frenzy by the maelstrom of thoughts and emotions coursing through her. I drew an arm round her to offer comfort and try to lift her beleaguered spirit.

"Hey, it's alright. You're not alone, *I'm* here. What did Grace say?"

"I...can't say. Sorry Luke," she said, detaching herself lightly from my arm, "It's not that I don't trust you; in fact it's *because* I trust you that I can't tell you."

I thought hard about what she had just said but couldn't make any sense of it – surely telling me would help me to help her, right? Why would her trust in me compel her to not tell me what had been said between her and Grace? It was clear Charlotte hadn't meant it maliciously – her tone and body language was enough to convince me of that, but still...

"That doesn't make sense," I uttered finally, highly baffled.

"It will in time. I'm sorry. Honestly."

"So...*what*? Am I supposed to twiddle my thumbs while Josh's life hangs in the balance?"

"Of course not. It's just that...things are *going* to happen, things that *I* have to change."

"Yeah..." I replied, still not grasping what she was driving at.

"So...if I tell you *everything* there's a chance your actions, however well-intentioned, could alter the timeline in ways I can't account for. It's causality – the ripple effects of one conversation or action can change the natural progression of a timeline. There's a chance you could be hurt and I don't want that. Please, trust me on this one."

"You sound like you've done this before."

"Trust me, after my conversation with Grace I never want to even consider time travel ever again; some things aren't possible for a reason! Luke, you're one of the best friends I've ever had, please don't feel like this is a reflection on you. I *do* need and want your help but there is only so much I can tell you. It's safer that way."

"I trust you but is there anything you can tell me? I don't want anything bad happening to Josh and I want to be at the top of my game when the time comes round."

"He's coming," Charlotte answered as she peered momentarily through the shop window, "I promise I'll tell you everything I'm able to later on. Meet me at third period – back of the art block."

"Alright."

The remainder of the walk to school was like walking on eggshells. All the way I kept pondering what it was that Charlotte felt she had to keep from me. Every crossing, speeding car and shady character along the way set me on edge as if at any moment fate could conspire with them to harm Josh. I knew I was being paranoid – especially as Charlotte had inadvertently shared the fact that Josh was safe until at least midday today by her choice of meeting time, but still – everything seemed to prove a catalyst for my anxiety of the inevitable. If I'm honest I don't think I've ever been as pleased to walk through the school gates as I was that morning – with previous perceptions of the school's overbearing aura of confinement giving way to a sense of relief at the measure of security from the outside world that the walls and gates offered. Josh was safe – for now.

Needless to say I was more than a little distracted all morning. Everything seemed to move around me like a blur while I remained in a solitary bubble of contemplation — so much was at stake right now — with Charlotte, Josh and Dad — that anything other than them didn't seem to matter to me anymore. In first period, which sounded vaguely like History, I doodled random shapes amongst keywords related to the objectives I felt needed to be achieved by my time here in 1990.

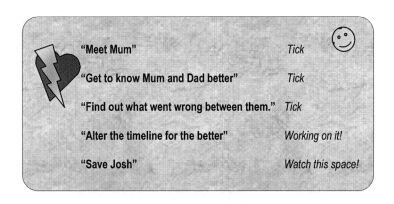

"Meet Mum"	*Tick*
"Get to know Mum and Dad better"	*Tick*
"Find out what went wrong between them."	*Tick*
"Alter the timeline for the better"	*Working on it!*
"Save Josh"	*Watch this space!*

I got shouted at a couple of times for not paying attention — momentarily lifting my head from the list and apologising before drifting back into my thoughts. Of course, by the time this happened the third time, the teacher attempted to make an example of me by giving me a surprise quiz on the topic she was lecturing on; and to be honest I think I stole her thunder a little bit. Luckily for me the topic was the Second World War and so all those hours spent watching war films and making models with Grandpa John paid off as I confidently answered all of the surprise questions — even adding in some extra information to some of them, leaving the teacher looking noticeably taken aback and somewhat embarrassed by her ploy backfiring.

When second period (Phys. Ed.) rolled around I opted to use the weights room instead of joining Ms (emphasis on the 'z') Phillips on the football field again. Ever since that incident with Collins, Phillips had come to view me as a nemesis – scowling whenever we passed each other in the corridor and picking up on miniscule things to criticise me on – ranging from the size of my tie's knot to the fact I usually wore trainers to school instead of formal shoes. Anyway, taking refuge in the weights room, I spent second period thinking over ways to help Dad while I ventured round the circuit of equipment at leisure – amused as ever by the active yet dated music pumping out of the portable cassette player in the corner – a mixture of commercial 80's pop and club classics.

I had to help get Dad motivated and make sure that he could stay strong after I went back to my own time – after all, I wouldn't get a second chance to come back. Everything had to be right first time. Encouraging him wasn't enough by itself – I had to make a hundred percent sure that nothing could steer him off course once I'd gone and that meant getting as much as possible stable in his life sooner rather than later. I was determined to fight for him – fight to ensure he had the chance to be the person and father he wanted to be. He was the reason I was alive after all – when Angie had wanted a termination, it was Dad who fought for me – now it was time to do the same for him. Coming here had shown me that though haunted by some deep emotional scars, James Hudson was a good man and one capable of bringing much happiness into other people's lives. Not just mine but Grandma and Grandpa's; Auntie Linda and Uncle Henry; Josh; the list went on. Helping him get the career he wanted seemed like the lynchpin of injecting stability into his life – it would allow him to do something he loves while being able to afford being a single parent.

That was what I had to focus on. He already had a terrific portfolio of artwork; he just needed a push in the right direction. As soon as I was able, I'd help him reach his dream.

A quick shower and ring of the bell later forced third period upon the campus of Lincoln Road High School – leading me to race across to the back of the prefabricated art block which, to be fair, more resembled a glorified portacabin than place of learning. Either I was early or Charlotte was late as I reached the meeting place to find it devoid of company. I paced up and down eagerly over a series of concrete paving slabs while I waited – the adrenaline and curiosity over what she'd say taking hold of me. Eventually after what seemed like a short infinity, Charlotte came rushing around the corner – smiling at me as she quickly caught her breath.

"Sorry I'm late," She panted lightly, "Just had to dodge my form tutor."

"It's cool, you ok?"

"Yeah."

"So...*what's* happening with Josh?"

Charlotte's expression straightened as her jovial smile simmered considerably.

"Field trip – two days time."

"How does it happen?"

"Not sure. I wasn't there originally, remember. I was off school with that virus from gym club."

"Oh yeah. Ok...well, we'll make sure *we're* there *this* time."

"Easier said than done, though. The trip is for design tech students only and neither of us take that class."

Crap! Yeah, that *did* complicate things alright. It was tricky but not altogether impossible. My mind began racing a thousand miles an hour with thoughts of every conceivable way of getting round this last minute snag until at last the answer came to me...

"It's ok, we'll go anyway – without them knowing." I announced at last.

"What?! How?! It's a factory somewhere in Essex – they're going by coach. There's no chance of stowing away – we'll be seen."

"Then we'll drive."

"Drive! Luke – we're *fifteen*!"

"Yeah...*here*. But back home I've got a full license. I know how to drive. And we could ask Grace for a car – surely an angel of destiny can rustle *something* up – after all, coming here was *your* destiny, right..."

Her face lit up – a vibrant shade of life flashed across her cheeks – prompting them to raise a satisfying, though unsure kind of smile. The optimistic glint in her eyes told me that she was considering the idea – running through the logistics of it as quickly as I had dreamt it up.

"It would work – *if* Grace goes along with it. She made it clear that she can't interfere."

"Well....she wouldn't be. Not *really*. She'd just be giving us what *we* need to interfere."

At that Charlotte perked up even more, visibly excited as her worries slipped away like shadows in the light. She hugged me unexpectedly – her touch reflecting the passion that was driving her efforts to save Josh.

"Thanks Luke. I'll go see if I can convince her. Could you cover for me here?"

"Sure. Tell Grace I say 'hi'."

"I will. Thanks...for everything."

*   *   *

The next day – the one before everything changed one way or another – both Charlotte and I were following our own agendas. She had skipped school with Josh in tow, having prepared a special day for the two of them involving a picnic lunch and day tripping around London. Meanwhile, I had also opted to avoid school for the day in favour of helping Dad with hunting for his dream job – meeting him at the flat before taking Luke to a neighbour Dad knew well and also heading off into the city.

We managed to catch a train to London Bridge straight from Sutton – and with the amount of inner-city stations it would have to pass through to get there, I had enough time to prime Dad for what he could expect.

"So Mr Hudson, what do you think you can bring to this job?"

"Huh?" replied Dad, confused.

I sighed.

"It's a practice question. If you fail to plan, you plan to fail."

"Mum says that." He answered.

"Yes, I know. She's said it to me so many times I probably recite it in my sleep. So...what do you think you can bring to this job?"

"Oh, right, erm...well...art has always been a passion of mine and I feel that I can offer a unique insight into adding value to the needs of any client's artistic requirements."

"Ok...not bad. Make them feel as if not hiring you would be a big mistake. Remember – it's mostly always a case of three things – confidence, charisma and passion." I nodded approvingly, "Now then...what do you have in the way of qualifications or experience in graphic design Mr Hudson?"

"I have an Art O level and a portfolio compiled over the last fifteen years of my best work. I've also made bespoke logos and stationery before now, along with custom Christmas cards for friends and family. Whilst not possessing a formal qualification in Graphic Design, I *have* honed my skills over a number of years and would consider any training opportunities made available to me."

"Your CV says you've mainly done office work before now, do you consider that a limitation to what you can offer to this job?"

"Bloody hell, Luke. Steady on."

"Come on, focus. You can't just *sneeze* your way into a job like this. You have to fight for it – just like you fight for anything else that's special to you."

"You really are behind me, aren't you?"

"Of course. James, there's SO much you can achieve if you just reach out for it and take the chance. You've settled for necessity up till now and any idiot can see it's making you unhappy so find a way to chase whatever dream you want."

"You sound like one of those motivation coaches that are all the rage."

"Nah, I've just seen a few too many talk-shows when suspended from school."

"You've been suspended?!"

"No, not here. I meant, *before*, you know...back home."

As quick as it had been, that moment where he'd registered compassion and expressed an interest stirred some part of my inner-child. All those years I'd acted out or just prayed that he'd get involved like a father should and now here we were – sitting on a rickety train carriage on our way into London at a time when I hadn't even been a year old in reality – and he embodied the very involvement I'd wanted for so long.

Suddenly the moment was shattered by sudden shooting pains in my head. It felt like one of those hardcore throbbing headaches that seems like a crap nightclub is in full-swing inside your head. My vision began to blur slightly as flashes of visions played out before me...

A birthday party – my birthday party. Banners and decorations scattered throughout a living room, but not one I recognised. "Happy 7th Birthday" the banners read. There were family and some friends from primary school there – my friend Joe who'd moved away to Devon when we were nine; Sophie – a girl in my year that I always used to play with at break-times; Dad – looking like the life and soul of the party; Grandma and Grandpa – both adorned in those cone party hats with the elasticised string. There was pop music playing in the near background – the kind that I'd probably never admit to ever having listened to. The lights went dim and a cake with seven blue and white stripe candles was brought in by – Josh! But Josh was blurry – so much so that I couldn't decide whether he was there or not. And then everyone sang happy birthday before Dad said to make a wish. I closed my eyes and blew with all my might...

*

When my eyes opened again I found myself on a sandy beach – in the middle of some kind of family holiday. Auntie Linda, Uncle Henry, Josh, Dad and me. It was a sunny day with a modest assortment those fluffy clouds floating overhead – all as white as a sheep's fleece, and the three grown-ups sat on a gathering of beach towels under a yellow and blue stripe parasol. Josh, looking slightly older than I knew him, threw an inflatable beach-ball towards me.

"Catch it, Luke." He said; his voice distorted slightly as if being tampered with by interference.

I began running for the ball, and everything grew progressively blurrier until the scene faded into white nothingness.

*

University graduation – Grandma, Grandpa and Dad all stood huddled around me while I, dressed in cap and gown, cheerfully held a scroll as the photographer took a group photo.

"Oh, Luke. I'm so proud of you." Grandma said, pulling me in close for a kiss.

"Well done son. I knew you could do it." added Dad, extending an arm around my shoulder and giving me one of those manly half-hugs.

And with that I was back in the train – in 1990 – sitting opposite Dad – the train shuddering as it changed track.

"Are you alright?" Dad asked.

The honest answer was 'no' but I didn't want to distract him from what he needed to do, nor did I want to have to try explaining the weirdness I was experiencing. What the hell *was* all that? None of that had happened – at least not the way it had been presented there. Was I daydreaming? If I was, I don't remember feeling sleepy or nodding off – everything had been normal before those pains had started. I couldn't explain it but I had to overcome it, or at least bypass it as best as possible for the time being.

"Just a little headache, it'll pass." I answered.

After that I continued quizzing Dad on potential interview questions for the remainder of the journey until we arrived at the bustling London Bridge station – negotiating busy commuters and manic pigeons to the exit. Even though we were here on business, it was still good to just spend some time doing stuff together. Who knows – if I get this right, maybe everything I'd ever known throughout my childhood would change. I didn't know for sure but just being here – now – knowing him as well as I did now and helping to make a difference seemingly healed the deeper scars left by his absence.

"Hey, how about after this I get us lunch or something?" Dad said as we shuffled through, past and around tidal flows of people in suits.

"How about Italian?"

Sweeping his dark grey suit jacket over one shoulder, Dad extended one arm around my shoulders as we walked towards his first interview. Knowingly blurring the context in my mind, I savoured every short moment as his words and touch finally made me *feel* like his son.

"I love Italian!" he replied.

I knew. Yet another thing we had in common; another link in the chain that connected us.

Chapter Twelve

Thursday rolled around quicker than Charlotte or I could keep up with and I don't think I've ever dreaded hearing the harsh tones of the alarm clock quite as much as I did that morning; knowing that there were only a handful of hours to change the course of history – to save a life taken long before its time and allow the future to benefit from that life's presence.

Josh had stayed at a friend's house closer to school the previous night so there wasn't even a chance for me to speak to him before fate and circumstance got in the way; and though dressed for school – attendance there today was the furthest thing in my mind as I briskly made my way to Artie's Cafe to meet Grace and Charlotte. Thankfully, Grace had agreed to our request – promising us the use of a car for the field trip. Brushing the double doors open forcefully, I stepped into the cafe to be greeted by the sound of a conversation stopping abruptly.

"Hey," I said, sensing the tense atmosphere.

"Hi."

"Morning Luke."

"What's...going on?" I asked.

"Nothing," Charlotte answered, "We were just going over what needs to be done."

She played absently with strands of hair – a thing she did when she was holding something back. It was clear that the two of them had been arguing before I'd arrived but as evident as that was the pair were eagerly trying to downplay or gloss over whatever had transpired between them. Something was going on – something that neither of them wanted to share with me; something that was obviously about the day ahead of us. But as curious as I was, my thoughts were with saving Josh – that had to take priority. Whatever was going on here could keep until later on.

"Right, well, we'd better be off if we wanna make that factory before 10. Where's the car?"

"Red Astra on the corner of Greyhound Road," Grace smiled as she threw the keys over towards me, "Now then, you'll have the illusion of looking like your adult selves to everyone else while in the car but you'll still be as you are now, so no drawing unnecessary attention to yourselves, okay?"

"Okay. Thanks." I answered, scooping the keys up in my right hand, "Right, let's go."

Charlotte remained silent as we hurried down towards where Grace had said the car was waiting for us. Sure enough we found a dull-red Vauxhall Astra sitting in one of the pay and display bays at the corner where Greyhound Road met the busy Sutton one-way system. Wasting no time, I unlocked the driver-side door and slipped in – reaching over to pull up the catch on the passenger side. Charlotte got in as I slipped the seatbelt on and began fiddling with the mirrors.

"Luke..." she uttered, still clearly troubled, "You know with your Dad, yeah? You'd do whatever it takes to make sure he's okay, right?"

"Well, sure." I answered, still tweaking the position of the rear-view mirror, "That's the whole reason I'm here. If someone means something special to you, you have to go all out for them. Charlotte, what's up? What's going on with you and Grace?"

"Nothing, it's just me being silly, that's all."

Whatever she was holding back didn't show any signs of being exorcised anytime soon and so rather than pressing the matter, I decided to just be there for her – safe in the belief that she'd tell me when and if she wanted to.

And so shifting the gear and releasing the handbrake, we drove away from the kerbside to start the most urgent race against time I'd ever come to be involved in.

We managed to make it through two sets of traffic lights before being stopped just short of the Post Office by a red light. I tapped the steering wheel impatiently while looking at the other lane of purring engines and frustrated drivers; and that's when I saw it. A metallic blue Ford Sierra Sapphire with a slick, yuppie driver – clad in his pinstripe armour and wearing that unashamed smug grin. In that instant I fell victim to a surge of red mist – seeing him that smug and self-assured stoked the fire burning inside me – the pain his and Angie's actions had caused stinging me like a thousand needles piercing my skin. The anger boiled inside until I felt it take control over my actions and as the red surrendered to amber I revved the accelerator in anticipation of the coming green light – making a sharp swoop at Simon's prized car and scraping against the remaining side where the paintwork was intact following my outburst the other day. But once wasn't enough – the anger inside refused to subside so quickly – and I found myself shunting into Simon's car again as the two of us kept pace along the dual carriageway.

"Luke, what the hell?!" exclaimed Charlotte.

"*That's* Simon. That's the guy Mum left Dad for. He's the reason the future becomes like it does. It's his fault – it's *all* his fault."

Eyes rippling with anger, I followed Simon like a fox chasing a rabbit – our cars running parallel like the course out destinies were taking. Neither giving nor gaining ground – a stalemate. As we worked our way around the one-way system, screeching past the turnoff for Cheam, Charlotte adjusted her seatbelt and turned to face me. She wore one of those empathic, almost motherly expressions that you couldn't help but feel disarmed by.

"Luke, let him go. I know what he did hurt you *and* your Dad but lashing out won't bring your Mum back – she made her choice. What matters is that you're here – now – for your Dad. What use will you be to him if you let yourself be consumed by this anger?"

"But I've been angry for so long, because of *this*, because of *him*. Anger is the only way I can release the poison I feel inside – it always has been."

"Then it's time to find another way. Trust me – anger will poison you even more – it'll mould you into whatever it wants and keep you cold to the people and things that really matter. That's how it got to me, right after Josh died."

"But we're changing that."

"Exactly...and *you're* changing things with your Dad. Things *will* change for the better but you've got to be at your best now, we both have; and that means letting Simon go. His actions will catch up to him in time, Luke. Don't let the anger blind you."

Charlotte's words resonated within me. I knew she was right – deep down I knew that what I was doing wouldn't achieve anything but it was like I had to fight against myself to regain control until reason overpowered emotion and I veered off into a backstreet next to Sutton Green – letting Simon speed off in a different direction while I pulled over and applied the handbrake before taking a deep, sobering breath.

My hands trembled with the adrenaline as I began reclaiming control of myself. It always happened like this. I was always left feeling ashamed of being so angry and scared that one day I might hurt someone involuntarily. I hated being so angry. I wished beyond measure that it was something tangible I could rip off or cut out – but it was like tar – thick, sticky and as dark as midnight's embrace.

"I'm sorry," I offered meekly as the war-drum beating of my heart slowed to a more normal rhythm.

"Don't be," Charlotte replied soothingly, "You're only human and love can make us do crazy things at times."

"The anger – it makes me a monster."

"You're not a monster, Luke, you've just had to put up with some crap situations that's all. Break the cycle – make a difference."

"You're right, thank you."

"Don't mention it."

Soon after we set off again – with a fresh perspective and me having left a haunting part of myself behind back on that one-way system. We passed through so many streets that I lost count. Where possible we stuck to main roads – only venturing into the backstreets of the suburban jungles to avoid traffic jams and road works with manual-operated "Stop-Go" signs that felt like an eternity to alternate. Charlotte diligently navigated the way, working from a street map she'd "borrowed" from her parent's car the previous evening; while I drove in rhythm to the music on the cassette tape we'd found permanently lodged in the stereo. If the reason behind the road trip hadn't of been so serious it would have been quite fun; but despite our motives the mood remained light and optimistic inside the car as we carried on journeying towards the factory where the Design Tech field trip had gone.

An accident on a major road near Romford delayed us for longer than either of us liked but thanks to some excellent off-the-cuff navigating and skilled driving (well, whizzing through the backstreets as safely as I could while Charlotte barked random directions) we made up for lost time, eventually arriving at the factory a little after quarter to eleven and parking within sight of the coach.

"Okay, *'Showtime'*." I said, pulling up the handbrake and turning off the engine.

Charlotte took a deep cleansing breath before opening the passenger door and exhaling some of the anxiety she had been bottling up for so long. She looked as if the weight of the world was on her shoulders but still managed to defiantly carry herself gracefully.

"Let's do this." She announced confidently.

From what I could see the factory looked like it produced furniture – primarily of wood. Large pallets of untreated wood stood at one end of the long car park near large delivery doors big enough to dock the trailer of a lorry. Venturing inside, we found the large industrial building to be a hive of machinery, noise and activity which we would have to navigate in order to find Josh. Of course, now that we were out of the car we appeared to everyone else as our fifteen year old selves again. Never before or since had youth been so complex!

We passed a series of machines all turning in clockwork synchronicity as if dancing to a mechanical beat – the cogs, pistons and other attachments all singing in tune to the chorus of industrial mass-production that reverberated throughout every square inch of the factory. Eventually reaching some of Josh's class, Charlotte wasted no time in getting straight down to business...

"Where's Josh?"

"What are *you* doing here? You're not in our class." answered one of the boys gathered near a restricted gantry.

Charlotte stepped forward – making her seriousness known with a stern expression and dominant body language. In fact, to anyone else Charlotte looked primed to explode with rage but I knew her better than that. She was channelling her anger – making it work for her instead of against her. Her assertiveness had shifted up a gear – determined to outrun the shadow of destiny that loomed so mercilessly over the one her heart belonged to.

"I don't have time to mess around Mike, now where's Josh?" she continued, raising her tone at the climax of the sentence.

The boy, noticeably taken aback, quickly lost his jovial grin and took a cautious step away from Charlotte.

"Whoa, Charlotte, relax...we all got split into smaller groups for the tour. We're just waiting for our guide – she forgot something in the office. Josh's group went off somewhere else – over near the timber processing area I think."

"Which way is that?"

"Over there..." replied the boy, pointing past Charlotte towards the right.

We set off at once. Thankfully the heavy automation of the factory meant less staff for Charlotte and I to dodge – making the journey through the labyrinthine factory a touch easier until, that was, we reached a T-junction on a strip of gantry where the surrounding mesh of machines moaned and hissed continuously.

"Which way?" I asked.

Charlotte looked at me intently but didn't answer. The tension went into orbit as both of us knew that making the wrong decision at this stage could allow things to turn out as they had done originally.

"I don't know." she replied, short of breath from the anxiety.

Suddenly, the sound of someone in trouble somewhere down the left fork of the gantry echoed just above the sound of the machinery – prompting both of us to nod in agreement before rushing off in that direction – hoping that we'd made the right decision.

The scared pleas got louder and more frequent the closer we got. It had to be Josh. It had to be. This was it. It all came down to this.

Arriving at a slightly wider section of the gantry we found Josh fighting to pull away from two nearby cogs that had begun feeding on his school tie. The two boys with him were instantly recognisable – Collins' goons – both of whom now stood frozen in terror as Josh desperately squirmed against the forceful embrace the machine had upon his tie.

"We didn't mean it. He was trying to get away. Tony pushed him and then..." exclaimed one of them.

"I didn't. It was him."

Despite their best efforts to pass the blame onto the other one, Charlotte and I sprung into action. There would time enough to figure out who had done what later on, what mattered now was saving Josh. Without hesitation Charlotte rushed forward – wrapping one arm around Josh and pulling him back with all her might whilst using her other hand to allow sufficient breathing space between Josh's neck and the knot of the tie.

"Wha...what are you doing here?" spluttered Josh.

"Saving your life now shut up!" she replied.

Acting as fast as I could, I ran back along the gantry to where I'd seen one of those thin fire extinguishers, ramming my elbow hard into the glass casing and ripping out the extinguisher as shards of tear-drop like glass continued to rain down from the top of the frame. I pocketed the largest and sharpest piece of glass I could see before rushing back to where Josh was – finding Charlotte struggling to keep Josh from being pulled further towards the unforgiving jaws of the timber processing machine.

"Hold on," I called.

Thinking fast and running solely on adrenaline I rammed the fire extinguisher into the machine – feeding it between the vice-like grip of the two offending cogs until the machine's grip was enough to freely support its weight independently. Within seconds the machine spluttered, hissed and let off a thin veil of light-grey smoke before grinding to a dramatic stop. A dull alarm tone then began passively filling the air as Josh exhaled as best he could now the force of the machine's pull on him had subsided. Charlotte continued her longing embrace on him while I withdrew the shard of glass from my pocket and used it to cut Josh's striped tie – frantically running across and deeper into the fabric until at last the jagged edges of the glass managed to sever the remaining few strands of fabric, leaving Josh to fall further into Charlotte's embrace.

Charlotte and I exchanged triumphant glances as we each caught our breath; the impact of our actions sinking in beneath the numbness of the adrenaline. We'd done it. Josh was safe. Disaster had been averted and destiny had been rewritten. Josh and his future had been secured.

Josh scrambled round and hugged Charlotte passionately – clinging onto her as if clinging onto life itself – his face noticeably awash with fear.

"I was going to...I mean, if you two hadn't been here...I..."

"It's alright. It's all alright now. I'd never let anything happen to you. I love you."

"I love you too."

Within minutes, the area had become a certifiable circus of activity – with technicians huddled around the machinery and the teacher in charge of the field trip looking more irate than a polar bear in the desert. When asked, Josh explained what had happened – how Collins' goons had followed him when he'd become separated from his group and had been pushing him around – literally – ending up in the disaster we had just narrowly averted. Needless to say the teacher read the two miscreants the Riot Act – promising all manner of ramifications once they got back to school, before turning his attention to me and Charlotte.

"You two shouldn't even be here."

"Yes sir" we said in unison.

"I should be reading the pair of you the Riot Act as well but seeing as it was your swift action that stopped me having to explain a student's death, I'm prepared to overlook your stowing away."

Needless to say we agreed and were allowed to stay with Josh and his group, albeit under the careful hawk-like watch of the teacher.

Woodwork had never been something I'd been particularly taken by. Don't get me wrong I had nothing against it; it's just that I just wasn't much good at it; but nevertheless this trip turned out to be fun. In fact, I remembered the time Grandpa had encouraged me to try making something out of wood. I'd aimed to build a birdhouse for the garden but it ended up looking more like a miniature (shell-damaged) tank. Of course, Grandma had been very diplomatic, stating – "Oh, that's nice dear, well done" before Grandpa softly added "What is it?!". Hmmm...Grandma and Grandpa – it felt like forever since I'd seen them. I missed them but I knew I'd be seeing them again when I eventually got back to my own time.

Anyway, nostalgia aside, it was great to see Charlotte finally relax and Josh still alive. In fact, all I needed now was to get Dad on-track and it'd be a full-house. Soon enough, the group stopped for lunch in the staff canteen – with small sub-groups and cliques spreading themselves to the four corners while they ate lunch. Josh, Charlotte and I chose a table near to the canteen counter as we had to buy something to eat. Preparing a home-lunch hadn't really been high-up on either of our agendas this morning!

"So, how come you two came along on the trip?" Josh asked once we'd all sat down.

"Well, Charlotte's been having recurring nightmares about something happening to you on the field trip so we decided to tag along – you know, just to make sure you were alright."

"You did *that* - for *me*?" he replied, gazing at Charlotte with puppy-dog eyes sweeter than a truck-load of pick-and-mix.

"I'd die for you, Josh Porter." She replied before nestling her head on one of Josh's shoulders.

The two shared another tender embrace as I turned my attention to my lunch to respect their privacy – the pair of them drawn to each other like the ocean waves kissing the golden shores.

"But...*how* did you two get here?" Josh asked after a few minutes.

"If we told you that we'd have to kill you!" I answered with a grin, looking up from my mostly eaten plate of shepherd's pie and beans.

Grinning also, Charlotte reached out and slapped my forearm playfully, "That's *not* funny!"

*   *   *

I left Josh and Charlotte alone for a bit after that. I figured they deserved some time alone to themselves without me trailing behind. Still, far from bored, I blissfully enjoyed the downtime of not having to worry about urgently changing something that had far-reaching implications. I listened to the guide as the group I'd been adopted by continued to tour the factory, with the euphoria of having saved Josh keeping me happily numb to stress. A fleeting gaze out of a staff room window some time during the afternoon alerted me to an absent space in the car park where a slightly battered red Astra had been, leaving me puzzled. I checked my pockets instantly – finding the car keys missing – having vanished as if they had never been there - the proverbial clock having struck midnight on this fairy tale. But the weirdness didn't end there...

Throughout the afternoon I began getting more shooting head pains, just like yesterday on the train, one of those nasty headaches that puts you off balance – you know the ones. But what was strange were the bizarre hallucinations that accompanied them...

Being back at my first day of school – dressed in crisp, pristine uniform on a chilly autumn morning. September 1995, I think. I was accompanied by Grandma Irene and...Dad.

"Daddy, I don't wanna go."

"It's alright. You'll have fun and I'll be back later to take you home." He replied.

The teacher – a middle-aged woman with thin, red-rimmed spectacles came to greet us with the widest smile I'd ever seen. The grownups talked among themselves before the teacher held out her hand for me to take hold of.

It was wrong. Dad hadn't been there. Grandma had taken me alone as Dad had given some excuse why he couldn't make it and I'd positively hated being left there. I remember having screamed and cried in protest – scared at not having anyone familiar around. But what I'd seen just now *wasn't* how it had happened. What the hell was that?

And another...

Christmas Nativity play in infants school. I'd been playing one of the shepherds and was on stage in the assembly hall. The hall felt huge and the spot lights overhead made the area around the stage feel really hot. Grandma, Grandpa and Dad were all seated about five or six rows back in the audience — Dad wielding one of those uber-large (at least by modern standards) camcorders gleefully. My costume consisted of a cape that Grandma had made out of fabric remnants she had and a tea-towel wrapped around my head — secured in place by a length of knotted string. After the play, Dad ruffled my hair playfully before picking me up.

"That's my boy." He said.

"Best little shepherd I ever saw." added Grandma.

Again, the devil was in the detail — things hadn't played out like that. Sure, I had been in the nativity play but Dad hadn't shown up after promising for weeks beforehand that he would. His absence had really gotten to me — so much so that it affected what should have been a memorable moment. I'd been so disappointed — so let down — that I'd forgotten the few lines I had, leaving me looking stupid and feeling embarrassed.

Just like before the hallucinations were fuzzy — like playing back a worn VHS cassette tape; but above all they were persistent — bleeding through with such clarity that they appeared like memories. But they were different — not how things had truly been. I'd have to ask Grace to be sure but I was more convinced than not that it was some kind of response to me playing around with the timeline.

When the trip was over, Charlotte and I returned to school on the coach — deriving much pleasure from seeing the teacher frog-march Collins' two goons into the main school building while the rest of us got to go home. With any luck they'd get what they deserved. I mean, they're actions had caused Josh's death, originally I mean. And even though Charlotte and I had intervened at the pivotal moment, it still didn't excuse what they did.

Still, that aside, the three of us made our way into town under the gaze of the orange late-afternoon sun. I guessed, though it hadn't been openly discussed, that we would be stopping at Artie's Cafe en route home. It all seemed so normal now but appearances can be deceptive and as we reached the one-way system we discovered how quickly things can change in an instant when the unexpected strikes...

It started out innocent enough – we'd pressed the button at the crossing and began walking across the road when the crossing began bleeping when suddenly, a car came racing around the corner much faster than was allowed. The driver didn't even attempt to slow down and I leapt out of the way – landing with a thud on the nearby kerb. I shouted out a few choice words I probably shouldn't repeat as I stumbled to my feet – still dazed and highly confused as I dusted myself off. Josh appeared next to me looking equally as dazed as I was.

"You ok?" he asked as he rubbed the back of his head.

"Yeah...yeah, I think so. You?"

"Same. How 'bout you Charlotte?...Charlotte?"

Josh and I turned round to find Charlotte lying in a heap a little further down the road on the opposite side.

"Charlotte!" Josh exclaimed fearfully.

We hurried over to her as quickly as possible – suppressing the pain either of us had sustained from our falls. I turned her over – finding blood trickling down her face from an impact wound – obviously where she had hit the car or ground or both. I didn't want to think about it but I had to do something. She spluttered after a few seconds before lightly panting for breath.

"Josh – go get help – that office over there is still open." I said, trying to think of what first aid I could do that would help.

Josh rushed off towards the nearby office block without question or objection – leaving me with Charlotte.

"Hey, it's alright," I lied, "Just try and stay still. Josh has gone for help – just hold on."

"Luke...it already *is* alright. Josh is safe." She said through laboured breath.

"Well, *yeah*...but..."

"I knew this was coming and I'm not afraid. Not anymore. I didn't have specific details or anything but...I knew something like this was coming."

"Wha...what are you talking about? You're not well – it's the shock."

"No Luke. *This* is what Grace and I were arguing about but I get it now. I understand. *This* is my sacrifice for making a big change to the timeline."

"But...that's not fair. You and Josh...you should be together. You came all this way. It can't end like this..."

"I've already spent a lifetime without Josh, Luke. I missed him every single day. The pain I felt – was more than one heart should ever have to bear. Where I came from, I was dying already – operating table – my heart gave out, probably from all the pain its harboured over the years. But this way I get to die for something...*someone* worthwhile. I've had several wonderful weeks with Josh and members of my family who weren't around anymore back home. Plus I got to meet you, so I'm not sad - not at all."

"Why? Why didn't you tell me? I could have helped you — we could have figured a way round this." I uttered, tears seeping from my eyes.

I didn't want Charlotte to die. It wasn't fair. She'd saved Josh — they should have had a long, happy life together. I just couldn't understand it.

"Because I *knew* you'd try and find a way around it. Either way *my* sacrifice equated to a life for a life and I didn't want to endanger yours. That *really* wouldn't be fair — you've still got your whole life ahead of you. I've had my time and at the end I got to do something wonderful with it. Luke, you've been the best friend anyone could ever ask for. I couldn't have saved Josh without you. Please understand that this has to happen."

Josh returned during the silent few seconds that followed Charlotte's explanation, accompanied by a receptionist and a security guard from the office block and flanked by a small selection of office workers who had come outside to see the commotion.

"Police and ambulance are on their way." said the young receptionist.

Understandably distraught and determined not to stray from her side, Josh cradled Charlotte as the blood from her wounds slowly began staining his sweatshirt while he began falling victim to a steady stream of tears.

"It's alright," he offered, running a free hand through her ruffled but otherwise perfect hair, "It's all alright."

As we waited for the ambulance Charlotte's breath became more erratic as her eyes began flickering in and out of consciousness – a sign that destiny was fast catching up to her. In a moment of laboured clarity, Charlotte lifted one hand to Josh's cheek and looked at him with a gaze that spoke every sentiment a heart could create.

"Josh, I love you so much and I always will."

Then, keeping her fleeting touch upon her sweetheart, Charlotte looked towards me with a triumphant smile as she uttered what were to be her final words, "I did it."

Chapter Thirteen

It was hard to forget that day – one of equal parts triumph and tragedy. I kept seeing that mortal scene pass before me over and over but I guess it must have been infinitely worse for Josh. In the few days that followed the tragedy, we were both allowed off school to (try to) come to terms with what had happened. Josh stayed in his room mostly – playing music to drown out the sobering reality of his sorrow. I wanted to say something...*anything*...that would make it all alright but I couldn't find the words.

I slipped out of the house on the second day – feeling unable to confine my thoughts and feelings to the same four walls anymore. Henry was at work, Linda had gone to visit a friend and Josh had fortified himself inside his room – only coming out when absolutely necessary. I wandered into town – guided more by inertia than thought, finding myself standing at the scene were the accident had happened. The lamppost nearest to where Charlotte had died was decorated with a collection of small fresh floral tributes while a yellow *"Can You Help?"* police board stood next to a section of pavement that still bore a faded dark patch of blood. Even as life went on around me I began to hear the accident echoing throughout - the car speeding; Josh's screaming Charlotte's name; Charlotte's laboured last words.

Pulling myself away from hearing the mental playback of the accident I walked the short distance to Artie's Cafe knowing that the only person I could talk to about this – the only person that would understand and have the answers I was looking for was Grace. The bell above the door chimed and jangled as I walked in – prompting Grace to emerge from a room behind the counter. She smiled warmly, her soft gaze offering every sympathy words ever could and silently beckoned for me to sit at the counter; and as I negotiated my way onto the retro chrome and red-leather counter stool Grace poured me a cup of white coffee garnished with chocolate sprinkles.

"I've been waiting for you. You must have a lot of questions."

"I don't even know where to start." I sighed.

"I know you must be feeling confused and probably angry at what happened..."

"Why didn't you tell me? Either of you? Why didn't either of you trust me enough to tell me she was going to die?"

I felt hurt, confused and so mixed up. All of this...*stuff* inside me felt like a volcano ready to explode. It was just too much to keep bottled away.

"Oh Luke," Grace sighed in a motherly tone, "It's not about trust. *I* couldn't tell you because I can't intervene like that – it was Charlotte's destiny and *she* had to make the decisions; and Charlotte didn't tell you because she was trying to protect you."

"Protect me? I don't understand."

"It's hard to explain but...I'll try. Imagine life as a *big* river, okay, and even though God and angels like me can help guide the path it follows, it can deviate on its own merits. The waters can stir and become violent; banks can burst; and the river can fork and snake off in different directions."

"*So*...what you're saying is?" I trailed, confused as I tried following her metaphorical explanation.

"What I'm saying is that if you had intervened and tried to save Charlotte then there was a chance — a *high* chance — that *you'd* have died instead. A river isn't fussy where it flows, what matters is *that* it flows. Does that make sense, sweetheart?"

"I think so. Sort of. I miss her, Grace."

"I know you do honey but it's ok, honestly, where she is now — she's very happy and in no pain whatsoever. She's safe — you have my word."

"Thanks Grace," I said before taking a reassured mouthful of chocolate-laced coffee, "Oh, yeah — I was gonna ask you — I've been getting weird headaches and hallucinations — you don't know anything about that, do you?"

"They're memories, honey." She replied as she walked over to wipe down some of the unoccupied tables.

"But they can't be," I said, turning round on the stool to face her direction, "I mean...those events didn't happen like I saw them. In fact some of them didn't even happen at all."

"But they will *now*. You see, all the changes you've been making here have started to take effect. What you're seeing are glimpses of the new timeline."

"Oh...*right*. But in some of the 'memories' — the first ones — Josh was blurry and out of focus somehow. What's that about?"

"That's because at that time Josh's fate was still in flux — still to be determined."

"One of those 'river' things?"

"Yeah." She smiled back.

A warm tingly sensation began consuming my chest – those visions were a future I'd helped to put right – they would all happen – Dad would be around and like he is here in 1990; Josh would be safe; we would all be a proper, functioning family – whole and uninterrupted. It was amazing, as if all the hope I'd poured into that birthday wish back in my time had been realised. Everything was going to be alright.

And then I thought of Josh – sure he had a whole life in front of him but right now he was still being swallowed whole by grief. He'd lost his first true love and that *had* to be a pain that weighs heavily upon any heart. I wanted to help him somehow but couldn't think of a way. But there had to be something...

"Grace, how can I help Josh? He's so upset. He's locked himself in his room since it happened and no-one can get through to him."

"Just do what you can. He needs all the support he can get right now. Wounded hearts are hard to heal and I guess it must be worse at his age. Just be there for him when he needs you, that's all you really can do. Everything has to happen when *he's* ready and not a moment before. When the time comes, he'll reach out to someone. But don't worry too much; Josh is part of my assignment here. Seeing as the destinies of you, Charlotte and Josh were intertwined as much as they are, I was sent here for all three of you – for you and Charlotte while you were here and for Josh after the two of you left. There are plans for Josh and I've been sent to make sure those plans still come to fruition in light of the changes to the timeline. I'll be here for him after you've gone home so don't worry – he'll still have someone to turn to."

That reassured me a lot. I knew I wasn't here specifically for Josh but ever since meeting him, I'd grown to like him – we *were* cousins after all; and that internalised mantra of family values cascaded into the dynamic between us.

The mention of home also got me thinking. I wondered how radically events and experiences I had gone through would change now. I knew it wouldn't be perfect but I wasn't expecting that nor searching for it – I just wanted to be part of a caring and cohesive family unit – where barriers weren't entrenched between you and those supposedly close to you. People will ultimately make some mistakes but it's all the stuff beyond those that really counts – deep down. Grandma Irene would undoubtedly still sneak off to have a crafty cigarette after telling Grandpa she'd given up; I would undoubtedly still get into trouble every so often; and Dad would most probably continue pining after Angie and putting that part of his life on hold for some time; but it didn't matter, not really, what matters is that we would be together; we would be a family. And even those not with us anymore still mattered in their own little way. Angie *was* still my mum and despite being angry with her for walking out on me and Dad, I still loved her on some level and wanted her to be happy. It is perhaps the hardest thing to describe but love is multi-faceted – it can bring people together and it can tear people apart. Deep down I wished I'd been able to keep my parents together but the realist in me knew that Angie was on a different path – her journey in life was taking her in a different direction to me and Dad. But still, I felt partially fulfilled – having been here and met her – *talked* to her. Those fleeting moments were the closest I had to a relationship with the woman that gave me life but somehow, given everything else, it was enough...*just.*

"Grace, can I ask you a really weird question, *please?*"

"Well, sure. What's on your mind?"

"Will my Mum be okay? I mean, Simon won't let her down or hurt her will he?"

Grace cast her warm gaze squarely upon me so that our eyes met on more than a physical level and offered a muted smile as she took a hold of my hands and squeezed them reassuringly.

"Sweetheart, you're Mum will be just fine. Simon really *does* love her and will always do his best for her."

"Will I ever see her again? In the future, I mean."

"I don't know. It all depends on the choices she makes. Free will is a difficult variable to predict. But even if your paths don't cross again don't let that stop you from being all that you can be, okay?"

Her words were uplifting and as soothing as the rain after a heat-wave. I suppose it was then that things made a bit more sense – that I *could* be angry with Mum and still love her at the same time. It was okay as long as that anger doesn't become what defines me. I guess getting some distance from a problem can sometimes be more productive than trying to fight it. Perspective, I guess, is in the eye of the beholder and having seen things with my parents firsthand I now knew the truth. I'd gained a different perspective – one that swept away all of the venomous doubt and speculation that had haunted me for so long. After all this time I was free of its cold, tar-like grasp and in control of that animal inside instead of the other way around. And *that* was what truly sets a soul free. It was liberating.

*   *   *

When I returned home a little after midday I heard someone moving about in the kitchen from the moment I stepped through the front door. Whoever it was sounded in a rage about something – as the sound of cupboards and drawers opening and being slammed shut boomed down the hallway. I cautiously stepped forward – unsure of who or what I'd find, until at last I emerged in the doorway to find Josh storming through the kitchen like a tornado. He looked like hell – dressed in night shorts and a grey singlet vest with hair that appeared as untamed as his mood.

He turned to face me – his eyes glazed over with the ferocity of a tropical thunderstorm and then, setting aside any previous thoughts of burglary, I realised what was going on. It was displacement; Josh was projecting his anger over Charlotte's death onto something tangible he could vent at.

"Josh? What are you doing? What's going on?"

"We don't have any bacon. Can you believe that? I mean, *what* kind of house *doesn't* have bacon?!" he answered, kicking a low-level cupboard in frustration.

"*Bacon*?!" I replied, raising an eyebrow, "You're tearing the kitchen apart for *bacon*?!"

"You don't get it. You don't understand!" Josh shouted, fury seeping from his every word.

Without warning Josh swung his forearm across the countertop, sweeping a fully-laden mug tree crashing onto the tiled floor below – the contents shattering upon impact.

"*Okay*...why don't we just calm down and..."

"I don't wanna calm down. I *want* her back," he replied as he pounded the fridge with a clenched fist, "I want her back...why won't she come back?"

As if a switch had been tripped, the anger in Josh succumbed to his undiluted grief – sending him slinking down the length of the fridge until he ended up sitting (sort of) on the floor – his head shielded by his hands.

I sat down next to him, leaning back against a cupboard. I didn't know what to say but in the end it didn't matter – he just needed someone there with him. No-one should have to face grief alone. I was here for him whether he wanted to talk or just wanted some company. As it turned out – he wanted both once he'd regained some measure of composure.

"I don't know what to do, Luke. Every time I close my eyes I see her and every time I open them I *want* to see her."

"It'll take time but eventually that pain will go away. Look, try thinking of it this way – when she needed you most *you* were there for her. She wasn't alone."

"But I couldn't save her, Luke. I had her in my arms and I couldn't save her."

"It wasn't your job to save her. What matters is that you were there for her – that she had you looking after her right to the end. Life is full of random crap like the other day but that doesn't mean you should stop living your life or enjoying it. Charlotte would *want* you to be happy. What would she say to you right now?"

"Probably to concentrate on the good things in life. Change what you can and overcome what you can't."

"Then that's exactly what I'll say to you now. Josh, don't let this anger define who you are or what you become. There's a whole world out there waiting for you and there's so much you can achieve. Live your life in memory of Charlotte – not mourning her."

"I love her so much. Even now. I just..."

"I know, I know. Sometimes we lose people close to us and it sucks but there are some things in life none of us can change and mortality is one of them. We've just got to do the best we can. You've still got people who are here for you, Josh. People who *want* to help."

"Yeah, I...just haven't felt like seeing or speaking to anyone the past few days."

"It's natural. You were in shock. But you can't shut yourself away – you've got to take each day as it comes – one day at a time."

Slowly, the barriers he'd put up after Charlotte died gradually came down. He became more open to talking and I stayed there with him – stayed there *for* him. I made him a cup of tea while I swept away the debris from the massacred mug tree and listened to everything he had to say. It wasn't long before he even started to smile again while twinkles of life began reforming in his eyes. The lights were well and truly coming back on. It was by no means a quick fix; he was still grieving and in considerable pain, but by easing it as best I could I hoped I was helping to alleviate the stress cast upon him.

With a fresh round of tea in hand the two of us ended up in the living room watching a film of Josh's choosing: a film that also happened to be one of my favourites – *"Ferris Bueller"*; as the dark grey rainclouds outside relentlessly hurled down lashing after lashing of rainwater. When Josh produced the video case I nearly laughed; it was so retro – well, to someone from my time anyway. Auntie Linda came through the front door, dripping wet from the gathering storm outside, just as the film studio's ident was playing. After saying hello, Linda went on to tell us that James would be joining us for dinner as he had some *quote* "good news" he wanted to share with everyone. Now, knowing that Angie returning was about as likely as Hawaii being snowed under, I guessed Dad's good news was the new job he managed to land; the last piece of jigsaw I needed to slot into place here in 1990. After briefly talking to us about dinner, Auntie Linda disappeared from view – leaving Josh and I to become engrossed in the movie. Man I *loved* this film, it never failed to make me laugh and, as I found out, it apparently held the same charm with my cousin too. Staying glued to the action for the entirety of the screening, we watched as the film played out; with Rooney making a complete arse of himself; Ferris outfoxing everyone whilst "seizing the day"; and the priceless moment when the classic car reversed through the garage wall - getting totally trashed on the forest floor feet below. Josh's mood continued to perk up throughout the movie – as if the humour was revitalising him – allowing him to see past his grief.

Anyway, the closing credits were rolling when the doorbell rang some time later, leaving me caught off-guard when Josh sprung into life to answer the door calling "I'll get it" in his wake. Josh's greeting made it clear it was Dad. I couldn't wait to see him – to congratulate him. He'd really come back fighting since Angie left. All being well, he was well on-track for staying a positive and *permanent* force in my life. Either way I was enjoying a part of a cohesive family – it was so seductive and yet so natural – like it was always meant to be this way.

I was just about to go and join Josh in greeting Dad when the TV flickered loudly with static – disrupting the still rolling credits of the movie until a face emerged against a blurry white background. It was Grace.

"Grace?"

"Hello Luke," she smiled.

"What are you doing...in *there?*"

"Well I couldn't exactly ring the doorbell."

A few seconds passed – allowing me to absorb some of the startling surreal scene unfolding before me – before Grace continued with what she had to say.

"It's time to go home."

"But...I *am* home."

"No. Home home. It's time to go back...or forward depending on how you look at it."

Sweeping aside the casual confusion at the use of tenses, I froze momentarily. I didn't want to go back – not now. I felt like I belonged here – I'd grown attached to the people I'd met here and felt genuinely part of something. I wasn't the angry guy I had been when I'd arrived. This place, these people had changed me for the better just as much as I'd changed the timeline and I didn't want to be separated from that.

"But Grace...I feel like I *belong* here."

"Luke, you've done what you came here to do. It's time to go home now. Come on...don't be afraid."

"But...my family..."

"...Will <u>still</u> be around in 2010. What about your grandparents? I know you're eager to see them again. Trust me – you've got a <u>lot</u> to catch up on."

I stepped into the hallway just as everything began to dim, except for the blurry light bleeding through the gaps between the kitchen door and the frame. Beyond the door I could hear the muffled enjoyment of Linda, Henry, Josh and Dad – all talking, all sharing a meal together. I wanted to be in there with them but I knew Grace was right. As much as I loved it here, it *wasn't* my time – *wasn't* my home. Soon, even the blurry yellow light began to dissipate into muted tones until it had enveloped me in translucent semi-darkness.

"But I never got to say goodbye."

"You didn't have to," came Grace's disembodied voice, "because they're all waiting for you."

Seconds later I began feeling disorientated as if I were falling and everything around me was constantly in clockwise motion. It felt like I was falling forever – on and on – down and down – as echoes of familiar people rang out – repeating parts of conversations I remembered and didn't at the same time. One of those "river" things I guess – the new timeline converging with my existing memories. I became so engrossed in absorbing the echoes and "new" memories that it took me completely by surprise when my back landed upon something soft – bouncing back up a few millimetres upon rebound. I blinked in bewilderment, finding myself in a bedroom – not my bedroom from Auntie Linda's or from my grandparent's house. So where was I *now*?

Shuffling off the bed and fighting the lingering sense of disorientation, I tried investigating my surroundings. There were knick-knacks, computer games and posters of things I liked; a laptop, _my_ laptop, sitting on a cluttered desk; and an assortment of photographs that apparently chronicled moments from a majority of my life – holidays, family events and school days.

It was all here – a record of a life I had yet to get properly acquainted with. Clearly this was supposed to be *my* room but where was 'here'?

But by far the biggest surprise was the bedroom door suddenly opening to reveal Dad, adorned with glasses and a jubilant expression. He was older, obviously, but still appeared fuelled by the same vibrancy I'd come to know him by in 1990. But it was what he said to me that really threw me...

"Morning son! Happy 21st birthday!"

Epilogue

"Dad? Where am I? Where is this?"

He laughed, stepping further into the room.

"Bloody hell, it *must* have been a good night. Have one too many last night, did 'ya? It's *your* room — you know, in the flat that we've lived in since nineteen-ninety-something. You sure you're okay, son?"

For a moment I struggled with what to say. I had to dodge telling him the time-travelling truth but even then, the honest answer to his question was 'yes' — I felt great — *here*, now. This was the future I'd worked so hard to put right and now here I was, and it was marvellous taking every second of it in.

"Yeah Dad. I'm fine, honestly. Just groggy, that's all."

"Okay, well, a cooked breakfast will be on the table in about ten minutes so err...better get yourself ready, eh birthday boy. There's lots planned for today."

The surprises just kept on coming and even though I knew this was all real, part of me couldn't believe what I hearing. Dad had never usually been around long enough to share a proper meal with before now, let alone *cook* one. It was all so strange. Grace had forewarned me that it would take time to adjust to the new timeline; and that it would be a bit disorientating at first counterbalancing what I knew from before with what was real now. Even so, disorientating or not, I didn't really mind. I felt at home and at peace like I was immersed in a very warm, very lucid dream.

"Don't look so surprised. Anyone would think I haven't cooked for you before." Dad said, evidently noting the bemused expression on my face.

Of course, he *hadn't* cooked for me before. I mean, the other Dad – from before. But that James Hudson and this one were thankfully worlds apart. *This* James Hudson was still the epitome of his 1990 self – brimming with cheer and compassion. I had to bury my perceptions of the old Dad; things here were different, I knew that, still it was strange adapting so radically to someone. Back in 1990 it hadn't been as bad – I didn't belong there so that James Hudson was a stranger to me, making it easier to get to know him. But here, now, this version of Dad was the polar opposite of the one I had left behind – the one that rarely bothered with me, even though I now knew his reasoning and although *this* version of Dad was awesome it was still bizarre to see such a change in someone I had known from here in my own time. Back in 2010.

"Sounds great Dad. I'll be there in a minute."

"You better be; or it's open season on the bacon!" he replied.

With that said, Dad left the room and I continued absorbing my new surroundings. Sitting on the bed I ran a hand through my hair as I laughed at how Dad's words echoed Josh's; bloody bacon! Unbelievable. *This* was unbelievable. It was a dream come true – and it had only just begun.

After a quick freshen-up I began investigating my new home before having to join Dad in the kitchen. The hallway was decorated in neutral colours and scented like vanilla thanks to one of those plug-in air fresheners by the front door; and adorned with framed pictures of me, Dad and the family.

*

Housed in a stained-wood frame was a large photograph of Dad and a woman both dressed in suits as they shook hands with a life-size mascot of a computer game character. Under the inner mount was a caption that suggested the picture had been in a magazine or newspaper.

"Some Work, All Play: James Hudson and Sophia Greene win award for their work on 'Rex Raptor 2: Extinction'."

*

Sitting on an end table alongside a cordless phone was a cheesy staged school photo of me around the time I started High School, along with a few others scattered throughout from different points in my school life. All cheesy and all doomed to a life in a dusty photo album or attic after they were taken down!

*

In a frame to match the other wall-mounted pictures, an enlarged holiday snapshot hung an equal distance apart from its counterparts. It was the beach I had seen in one of those memory flashes – a shot of Josh and I playing with an inflatable beach ball as the surf swept over our feet and the sun kissed our skin radiantly. From the looks of it I must have only been about two or three but a residual feeling of happiness swept over me.

"Memories" came flooding back to me as I continued to gaze at any pictures I could find in the hallway and living room. It was as if I were somehow absorbing the new memories from them. Weird. I guess Grace would have said something about a "cascade effect" or some other fancy time-travel description but let's just call it one of those 'river' things and move on. There were so many memories that it was like absorbing a whole new lifetime: moving into the flat after Dad and I had stayed with Grandma and Grandpa for a bit; the October we had a massive power cut and had to live by candlelight for a fortnight; summer holidays spent going places (even abroad) with Dad and sometimes others as well; Josh becoming a paramedic; and Dad going from strength to strength in his career – even going so far as to go into partnership with another graphic designer and forming their own design studio.

But before too long, the mouth-watering smell of the cooked breakfast finally tempted me into the kitchen where I found Dad waiting for me at the modest beech-wood dining table. A purple envelope was propped up against a steaming mug of coffee.

"Happy Birthday Luke."

"Thanks Dad."

Taking my place at the table, I opened the envelope to discover a birthday card – one of those ones with an innocent black and white photo alongside a humorous tagline.

"To Luke. Wishing you a happy 21st. Am so proud of you, son. Love, Dad."

There was so much I wanted to say but somehow it didn't seem necessary. I had literally waited all my life to know that I actually meant something to him and to hear those words; and now here they were – written right in front of me. Everything was as it should be and as it always should have been; and so my story ends where it began...*sort of*; on my 21st birthday – the one that *did* happen.